D0985855

Bra X
Bradford, Laura
Jury of one

1st ed.    OCT 1 6 2006

LAP
$16.95
ocm60587400

WITHDRAWN

# JURY OF ONE

## Laura Bradford

HILLIARD HARRIS

P.O. Box 3358
Frederick, Maryland 21705-3358

This novel is a work of fiction. Names, characters, places and incidents either are the product of the author's imagination or are used fictitiously. Any resemblance to actual persons, living or dead, events, or locales is entirely coincidental.

Jury of One  Copyright © 2005 by Laura Bradford

All rights reserved. No part of this book may be reproduced or transmitted in any form  or by any means, electronic or mechanical, including  photocopying, recording, or by any information storage and retrieval system, without the written permission of the Publisher, except where permitted by law.

First Edition-June 2005
ISBN 1-59133-094-7

Book Design: S. A. Reilly
Cover Illustration © S. A. Reilly
Manufactured/Printed in the United States of America
2005

To Mike, for always believing I would soar,

And to

Erin and Jennifer Lynn, for being the sunshine in my days.

I Love You.

# Acknowledgements

My sincere gratitude to Art Cummings, whose support and guidance helped turn my childhood dream of writing into a reality. And to Police Chief Steve Talbott, for taking time out of his busy schedule to help make my police talk a little more "hip". And to Chuck Schlie, whose enthusiasm for this manuscript kept me going.

My heartfelt thanks to "Jackie's mom", for helping to re-ignite my passion for writing fiction, and for being a huge source of encouragement throughout the writing of this book.

And last but not least, much thanks to my editor, Shawn Reilly, for fulfilling a lifelong dream the day she accepted, Jury of One. Thanks Shawn!

# I

## 8:45 p.m.
## Monday, June 7


It *had been* one of those days that made him doubt his decision to become a cop. Where were the opportunities to make a difference? Where was the excitement? Where were all those heroic reasons his dad had felt were worth dying for?

Surely it wasn't in the stack of paperwork he had spent the past three hours working on, or the petty theft cases a preschooler could solve. And it sure as hell wasn't in the courtrooms where perp after perp got off because they were so and so's second cousin removed.

Mitch Burns exhaled slowly and ran his hand through his hair. One thing was for certain. Now was not the time to spend soul-searching. His head was throbbing and the only thing that could stop it was a plate of food. A *huge* plate.

Fortunately for him, the answer was just a few steps away. Mia's Chinese Food could cure just about anything, including the Monday blahs. In fact, he found it funny how his stride quickened at the same spot every week.

The string of bells above the door jingled as Mitch pushed his way into the dimly lit restaurant. His head was starting to feel better already.

"Hi, Mia, how ya doin' this evening?" He leaned across the register and kissed the woman's gently lined forehead. A hint of soy sauce on her skin made him smile. No matter how long the day had been, somehow it always seemed insignificant when he stepped inside her restaurant. Maybe it was the inviting smells or the genuine smile she always had for him. Maybe it was the knowledge that despite a hard life, she was always positive and upbeat. Or maybe she was one of the angels on earth Aunt Betty always spoke about. He squeezed Mia's hand and smiled.

Her dark eyes searched his face closely. "I am fine, but you look tired, Mitch."

And she could read him like a book.

"I am. It's been crazy around the department the past few weeks." He leaned his weight against the counter and traced a faint crack along the muted gold Formica with his index finger. "The chief's a bit on edge these days with a new boss to answer to. And when the chief is on edge...look out."

"I take care of you, Mitch. Cashew chicken, white rice and egg roll?"

"Predictability probably isn't such a great personality trait for a detective, huh?"

"You good detective. I just know your favorites."

"That you do. Thanks, Mia."

There was something comforting about living in a town where people knew you. Your likes, your dislikes. Now if only a few available women would move in, Aunt Betty would be thrilled. And frankly, so would he.

A copy of the latest Ocean Point Weekly waited for him on his usual table. He sat down, draped his leg across an adjacent chair, and unfolded the newspaper with casual interest. The front page was fairly predictable; an article on the new mayor, a photograph of Dave and Pat's kid with another spelling bee trophy, and...

His shoe hit the ground with a thump as he sat up straight in his chair. The headline was a dead giveaway. Johnson and Associates was at it again. Although his eyes read the words in front of him, Mitch's head practically wrote the story. And it was the same old thing it had been last year. And the year before that. Good old Danny boy Johnson was trying once again to win support for his proposed luxury condominium complex.

The thought of more vacationers squeezing into Ocean Point, New Jersey, each summer was not Mitch's idea of fun. More tourists meant more problems, and more problems meant more work for him and everyone else in the department.

As he turned the page, Mitch's eyes fell on the small headshot of an attractive young woman. Wishing the photograph was in color, he found himself eagerly reading the brief biography that accompanied it.

*Elise Jenkins, 22, has joined the editorial staff of the Ocean Point Weekly. Jenkins graduated this spring with a*

2

*Bachelor's Degree in Journalism from the University of Missouri. Jenkins will be covering both news and feature stories in and around the Ocean Point community.*

Aunt Betty's prayer group must have been praying hard lately.

He looked again at the young girl in the picture. Wavy dark hair, high cheekbones, beautiful lips and a killer smile.

"She pretty, Mitch."

Damn it! Apparently *hearing* wasn't one of his strong points either. He turned the page quickly. Slowly, he raised his head and looked up at Mia, furrowing his brows as convincingly as possible. "Who's pretty?"

"Now Mitch, I see you look at picture of new reporter. It be our little secret, no?"

So much for his acting debut. He prayed silently for the ground to open up and swallow him whole. Barring that, he would simply settle for his face to return to its normal shade.

"Now don't go being shy. You need someone special in your life."

"You've been talking to my aunt, haven't you?" he said, knowing full well there was no sense in arguing. Aunt Betty was always after him to "find a nice girl". It was best just to nod stupidly.

He cleared his throat and pointed at the plate of food the woman held. "That looks great, Mia."

"You can change subject, but you know I right," she said quietly. She carefully set his plate on the table in front of him and then headed back to the kitchen.

Trouble was he *did* know she was right.

With a determined sigh, Mitch reached for the chopsticks Mia had placed beside his plate. Carefully crossing the bottom portion of the wooden sticks, he triumphantly picked up a small piece of cashew chicken. As he moved the food toward his mouth, small tremors vibrated his fingers, wrist. And like clockwork, the chicken fell into his lap. Too hungry to try anymore, he reached for the fork Mia always left for him "just in case."

It didn't take long for the food to work its magic. The headache that only 30 minutes ago had seemed like it would never go away was disappearing almost as quickly as the food on his plate. And, like any good medicine, it cleared his thoughts of all things bothersome. Including paperwork.

The crackle of his radio snapped his attention back to reality.

"D-1, do you copy?"

He grabbed the radio from its holder and held it to his mouth.

"D-1. Go ahead."

"We've got a human J-4 at 115 Sea Wave Drive. Suspicious circumstances, please respond immediately."

"D-1 in route," he answered quickly.

Mitch Burns stuffed the last bite of egg roll into his mouth and leapt to his feet. His heart pounded in his chest. A suspicious death in Ocean Point? It was almost too hard to believe.

"Gotta go, Mia. Duty calls."

### 9:55 p.m.

Nothing at the academy could have prepared him for this moment. Sure, he had seen dead bodies before, but in Ocean Point they usually belonged to 80-year-old nursing home patients. Not young women in their mid-twenties.

He made a mental note of the victim's fully clothed body. Not a rape. Her car keys were still clutched in her left hand, her hair matted with blood. A botched burglary?

He bent down and studied the woman's body, his eyes stopping on her right hand. The index finger was fully extended. How odd, he thought.

"She must have been nagging some poor guy when she bought it, huh?"

Mitch turned to see Troy, the department's rookie, standing behind him.

"What are ya talking about?" Mitch asked, his voice dripping with irritation as he once again turned back toward the victim.

"Her finger. My wife shakes her finger at me like that all the time when she's nagging me about something. But then again, you're not married, so you haven't had the pleasure yet, have you?"

It was amazing how there always seemed to be enough females around for a loser like Troy.

"Any sign of forced entry?" Mitch knew his question was biting in tone, but he had little use for guys like Troy. They were so used to their cocky frat-boy attitude getting them places in life. But it wasn't going to fly with him.

"Nope. Looks like the perp walked through the front door just like your average Joe."

Mitch reached into his shirt pocket, pulled out a tiny recording device and stood up. He walked around the body and knelt beside the woman once again. A tiny sliver of wood near the woman's head wound caught his attention. He pushed the *record* button and began speaking.

"Female victim. Mid-twenties. Body discovered by a neighbor. Face down. Looks like she was hit with some sort of wooden object to the back of her head."

He looked around at the small apartment.

"Victim found in her kitchen. No sign of a struggle."

An open door at the end of the hallway obviously led to the woman's bedroom. He stood and walked the short distance to the neatly kept room. A wooden jewelry box stood on the dresser to the left of the bed, several necklaces visible through its small glass opening. A bank envelope nearby contained a withdrawal slip and ten crisp twenty dollar bills.

Mitch raised the recorder to his mouth once again and spoke slowly and clearly.

"Money, jewelry, possessions seem to be untouched. Robbery does not appear to be the motive."

When he walked back into the kitchen he was relieved to see that the officers assigned to fingerprint and photography detail had arrived.

"Hey, guys, thanks for getting here so quickly. And, Sorelli, make sure to get lots of shots of the victim from every conceivable angle. Thanks."

He turned his attention back to the victim's immediate surroundings. A woman's purse sitting on top of the coffee table in the cheerfully decorated living room caught his eye. He reached into the leather bag and pulled out the woman's wallet. The driver's license put a name to the victim's face.

Susie Carlson. 24 years old.

"Mayor Brown is *not* going to be happy with this one," Troy said, looking over Mitch's shoulder at the license. "With the tourist season hitting full swing next week, this could certainly put a damper on things."

"Right now I'm a bit more concerned with who killed this girl and why," Mitch said. But he knew Troy was right. A brutal murder at the start of vacation season could send a panic through town. A panic that could disrupt the kind of business that Ocean Point relied on to survive. There was going to be a lot of pressure on the department to solve this crime quickly. And as the department's only detective, the brunt of the pressure was going to be on him.

He ran his hand across his eyes and then over his hair. One of the main reasons he had decided to pursue police work was finally at his doorstep in a very big way. Some slime had decided to take an innocent woman's life. And in that same split second he had ruined an entire family.

Mitch leaned against the wall and closed his eyes. His mom's tear-streaked face filled his mind. It was the not knowing that had killed her. And Mitch wasn't going to let that happen to another family. Suddenly, the pressure he was going to get from the department to solve this crime paled in comparison to the pressure he knew he was about to put on himself.

His gaze drifted out the window to the coroner's vehicle that had just pulled up to the curb. Mitch stepped out onto the screened-in porch and held the door open for the man and his gurney. "She's in the kitchen."

The coroner stopped to shake Mitch's hand then followed him down the tiny hallway toward the kitchen. "So, what do we got here, Mitch?"

"Female victim, 24 years old, wood splinters near the head wound..."

"Oh my God, Mitch, that's Ray Carlson's daughter."

The kind face belonging to the organ player at St. Theresa's suddenly filled Mitch's mind.

Pressure wasn't the word.

# 2

## 4:30 p.m.
## Thursday, June 10

Elise Jenkins studied every detail of the photograph in her hand. All the legwork she had done over the past two days had painted an image of Susie Carlson that made her murder even more unexplainable. The young woman had been the pride and joy of every teacher she had, every coach who worked with her, every neighbor she had touched. And, based on the picture Elise held, the victim had been someone who was absolutely adored by her younger brothers and sisters.

The image captured Susie during the Christmas season. Her pretty blonde hair was twisted into a French braid, her big brown eyes a complement to her infectious smile. She was tickling a younger girl with one hand while her other arm rested casually across the shoulder of a young man who looked a little younger than Susie.

"It's sad, isn't it?"

Elise wiped at the tears threatening to spill down her cheeks and looked up from the photo. Debbie, the office receptionist, peered over her shoulder, a frown tugging at her lips as she looked at the picture.

"I can't even begin to imagine what her family is going through right now." Elise cleared her throat in an effort to make her voice stronger. "I never thought I'd be facing a story like this so early."

Debbie softly touched her shoulder. "You'll do fine."

She hoped Debbie was right. But ever since the photograph had been dropped off at the paper, all Elise could do was stare at the victim.

Reluctantly, she set the picture down and turned back to her computer. The cursor on the darkened screen blinked at her, a reminder that she had stories to write. One of which might very well be the biggest story of her writing career.

"How's it going, Elise?"

She looked up to see her new boss, Sam Hughes, standing beside her desk. His balding head was deceptive, leading people to believe he was much older than 40-something. But when it came to his personality there were no mistakes to be made. Sam was one of those people that everyone instantly liked. Straightforward yet sensitive. Humorous yet serious. And, most importantly, he understood her passion for writing.

"Okay, I think. You know something?" She took a breath and continued on, not waiting for his reply. "When I used to dream about being a reporter one day, I figured I was a bit unrealistic when I would picture my first assignment being full of suspense and danger. I guess it wasn't so far fetched after all, huh?"

He nodded his head and perched on the edge of her desk. "I know exactly what you mean, Elise. I thought I'd be breaking you in with something like a street repair or a school board meeting. But I've got faith in you. You have the desire to tell a story and the heart to tell it compassionately. And that's a rare combination, a winning one in my book."

And there it was. The motivation to do the best job she could. If only her parents could have such genuine faith in her and her writing ability.

But that wasn't going to happen anytime soon.

Her mother's words echoed in her ears. "Why don't you get into public relations or advertising...at least then maybe you can actually eat once in a while and have a real life."

But it wasn't about the money. It was about the ever-changing stories, the constant challenge, the interesting people she would surely meet along the way. They just didn't get it. And they never would.

But Sam got it. And she was determined to make him proud. She just needed to find a way to keep the self doubt at bay long enough to convince her parents and everyone else that she had what it took to cover a murder investigation. And if she proved something to herself along the way, that would be even better. But she had to get rid of her headache before she could do anything else.

Elise pulled a bag of pretzels from the bottom drawer of her desk and permitted herself a five-minute break. She had been going non-stop all week, savoring every moment of her first few days on the job. She was glad she had stuck to her guns and searched for jobs as far from Missouri as possible. Ocean Point, New Jersey was a perfect place to start her new life as an adult.

It hadn't taken her long to see why the small ocean-side town was a favorite vacation spot for thousands of people each summer with its clean beaches and family style entertainment.

There was something so refreshing about being near the ocean. And, at the end of a long day spent soaking up rays and playing on the beach, it was hard not to be beckoned to play by the two amusement piers on the southern edge of town. The combination of rides, games, and fortune tellers had proven to be a winning one for the vendors who set up shop there each year.

Elise leaned back in her chair and popped a pretzel in her mouth. She had struck gold with her apartment. The one bedroom unit was just a short walking distance to the beach and the landlord had given her permission to paint and decorate to her heart's content.

But she needed money to do that. And Grandma's graduation check was just enough to survive two weeks in her new apartment before starting at the paper. It had given her time to relax, get organized, and work on her tan. Her evenings were set aside for pouring over back issues of the Ocean Point Weekly that Sam had given her after she accepted the job.

Elise had made a point of studying any and all photographs she saw that contained the key players in town...an effort she hoped would pay off when the job actually began.

When her first day at the paper had finally arrived, Elise had felt more than ready to face whatever challenges came her way. And then the murder happened. She was totally unprepared for the story that would be placed on her lap when she walked into work on Tuesday.

Somehow, she had to put everything she had learned at college into action and write about the murder of a girl just two years older than she was. But she knew one thing for sure; she was going to cover this murder with decency. She would prove to everyone that journalists can write with compassion and understanding while still providing the facts. It had been the driving force behind her choice of careers ever since her aunt's accident and the trial-by-fire her uncle had gotten from the press.

Elise shook her head softly and forced herself to concentrate on the screen in front of her. She didn't have time for self-reflection. She glanced again at the picture beside the keyboard.

No matter how much legwork she had done before her first day on the job, nothing could have prepared her for the emotional toll a story like this would take on her. But, then again, it really shouldn't have come as a surprise. Ever since she was just a little girl, Elise had been sensitive to the pain of others.

And, for some reason, much like a moth is drawn to the flame, Elise felt compelled to uncover the reason for people's sadness and to somehow find a way to try and ease it. Fortunately for her, Sam seemed to be a similar creature and respected her desire to give the police a few days before hounding them with questions for which they had no answers yet.

But the time had come for the phone call to the police. She had given them nearly three full business days without questions, and she couldn't give them any more.

She reached for the telephone on her desk and dialed the number of the Ocean Point Police Department.

"Hello, this is Elise Jenkins with the Ocean Point Weekly. May I please speak with the detective in charge of the Susie Carlson case?"

She twirled the phone chord around her finger and waited to be transferred to the correct person.

"Detective Mitch Burns. What can I do for you, Miss Jenkins?"

"Elise, please," she said. She wished her voice didn't sound so nervous, so young. "I'm working on deadline right now and I wanted to see what kind of developments you may have for me in the Carlson murder investigation."

"Nothing to report at this time, but we're examining every piece of evidence from the crime scene and we will find the person who did this. Now, if that is all, I have work to do."

She tried to remind herself that it had to be a stressful time for a detective, but she couldn't hide the irritation she felt by the shortness in his tone.

"That's it for *now*, Detective, but I *will* be following this case closely."

She hung up the phone with authority, aware of the anger building inside her. She had given the police almost three full days without questions, working off a basic description of the crime from some department intern! Did the detective not realize how most reporters would have been in his face the second the body was found?

"Hey, Elise.  Susie Carlson's obituary just came over the fax line for you," Debbie yelled.  "You wanna see it now?"

Elise pushed back her chair and walked over to the receptionist's desk.  It hadn't taken long to realize that Debbie was the eyes and ears of the office.  She was up on everything going on around town and at the paper.  So it was no surprise when Elise found her reading the obituary with rapt interest.  It was hard to get mad at Debbie when she listened to conversations that weren't intended for her or looked at faxes that had someone else's name on it.  She was simply a curious person, a trait that came in handy in a newspaper office.

Elise leaned over Debbie's shoulder and skimmed the notice for anything that might be helpful.  Some of the information she had already obtained, other parts were new.

Out of college just three years, Susie had been pursuing a career in accounting at a firm in nearby Montville.  She was one of five kids and had been born and raised in Ocean Point.  The funeral Mass was scheduled for tomorrow at 10 a.m. at St. Theresa's.

"Thanks, Debbie."

Slowly, Elise walked back to her desk and sat down.  She needed to focus her attention on the other stories she was working on for tomorrow's deadline.  But somehow stories about the new mayor's park proposal, a developer's drive to build luxury condominiums, and the chief of police's request for more manpower seemed so trivial compared to the town's first murder.

She had to tell the story of the murder itself, but she also wanted to tell people about Susie Carlson.  A young woman who was loved by everyone she touched.

As she looked again at the photograph of the young woman, just two years her senior, Elise decided that the funeral might be a great way to gain more insight into who Susie Carlson really was.  And then maybe, just maybe, she could finally go about the task of turning a horrific story into something she could be proud of.

# 3

## 11:00 a.m.
## Friday, June 11

It *was hard* not to stare at the victim's family. They looked so sad and lonely as Father Leahy spoke to each one of them from the altar. Mr. Carlson was obviously trying to be the rock of the family as he kept a protective arm around his wife throughout the service, yet those strong shoulders were unable to disguise the emotion he experienced at the priest's reference to Susie as "Daddy's little girl".

Mrs. Carlson looked down at her hands often throughout the service. And, after awhile, Elise finally figured out why. A small photograph was clutched in the woman's left hand; a photograph Elise assumed must be of Susie. The youngest of the Carlson children kept looking at the mahogany casket, a look of disbelief evident in each uncertain glance.

"I would like to invite Michael up to the altar to share a few words about his sister." Father Leahy stepped out from behind the lectern and extended his hand to a young man with auburn hair and tear-filled eyes.

Elise recognized Michael from the photograph she had received at work. It had been evident to her even then how close the two seemed to be and her heart broke for him. She found herself choking back tears as she watched him struggle to gain enough composure to speak to the crowd of people who had come to pay respect to his dead sister.

After what seemed like an eternity, the young man began to speak. "I'll never forget the time when I decided to pick on someone in my class because all my friends were." The quiver in his voice was unmistakable, causing sniffles and soft crying sounds to emerge throughout the church. "When I got home that day, I felt a little guilty about what I had done. I told Susie about it and she told me something that has stuck with me ever since. She told me that it's easy to tease someone because everyone else is, but it takes a better person to tell them to stop."

Elise grabbed for her purse and fished out a tissue. She wiped at her eyes and nose. It was becoming harder and harder to swallow over the lump that was growing in her throat. She thought about her own high school years and the teasing she had endured for being a "goody two-shoes". If only she had come across someone like Susie Carlson. Maybe she wouldn't have had to doubt herself so much.

"It was like that all the time with Susie," Michael continued, his hands gripping the sides of the lectern as his eyes rested on his parents. "I was terrified to go to high school. It seemed like such a big place after grade school. Most of my friends were switching to the public school so I felt really alone. When I got to school that first day, Susie and her friends made room for me at their table in the lunch room so I wouldn't have to sit by myself. How many big sisters would do that for their kid brother?"

Elise looked up at the ceiling of the church and steadied her breathing. If he didn't stop talking soon, she was going to burst into loud sobs. She could feel it coming. She counted to ten, forcing her mind to think of something, anything, besides the young man's heartbreaking words. She looked back at Michael who had grown silent.

He pointed to a young girl in the third row.

"Maureen, you were such a wonderful friend to Susie for as long as I can remember. She truly loved you with her whole heart."

Elise saw the corner of the young woman's mouth turn upward in a trembling smile before she dissolved into uncontrollable sobbing.

Elise swiped quickly at the tears that escaped her own cheeks. She remembered when a "Susie Carlson" had entered her own life. And she knew all too well how much it hurt when she slipped away. It was a time she never wanted to relive.

The organ began playing the first few notes of the closing song. Michael joined five other pallbearers who hoisted the casket onto their shoulders and carried Susie out of the church.

Elise tried to sing but her voice sounded weak and raspy. Instead, she watched Susie's loved ones as they followed the casket down the aisle, grief etched into the face of everyone she saw.

When the procession finally made its way to the back of the church, she grabbed her handbag and headed for one of the side exits.

She had to pull it together if she was going to be able to interview anyone.

As she stepped out into the brilliant sunshine, she came face to face with the town's new mayor, Steve Brown. His closely cut hair had obviously been black at one time, as a few reminders of his youth peeked through the silver that virtually covered his entire head. Piercing brown eyes searched and examined every face he looked at. The pictures Elise had studied of him prior to their first meeting at City Hall hadn't done justice to the commanding presence he emitted in person.

"Good morning, Mayor Brown."

"Miss Jenkins...good morning to you, as well."

"Could you please give me a statement on this horrible tragedy?"

"Certainly. The entire community of Ocean Point is grieving along with the Carlson family today as they prepare to lay their beloved daughter to rest. What a horrible shame this all is to her parents."

"Thank you, Mayor." Elise scanned the crowd looking for another quote. She could feel the lump in her throat dissipating as she focused on her work.

Her eyes fell on the town's police chief. With several quick strides she found herself face to face with the tall uniformed man she had seen only in pictures. The small moustache that looked so professional in photographs, made him look almost sneaky in person.

"Chief Maynard, I'd like to introduce myself. I'm Elise Jenkins, the new reporter for the Ocean Point Weekly."

The tall, burly man smiled easily and extended his hand to her. "Welcome to Ocean Point, Elise. I wish your first week could have been a little more calm."

"You and me both." The grin that stretched across her face felt good. She only wished that the Carlson family could smile again soon. "I was hoping to get a statement from you about the Susie Carlson murder."

"Sure thing, Elise. What happened to Susie Carlson this week is unforgivable, and we will work day and night until we've found the person who committed this horrific crime."

"Thanks, Chief."

"One more thing. I would like to point out that this crime, although a first in Ocean Point, is one very good example of why we could use some more police officers on the beat," the chief said. "We are a town that relies on our summer tourism quite heavily, and it would be very short-sighted of us to risk that much-needed income because we don't want to properly staff our police department."

Elise jotted down the chief's comments then noticed that he was looking around the church grounds as if searching for someone in particular. His hand suddenly shot up in a beckoning gesture. She tried not to stare, but the man walking towards them was quite good looking in a confident, athletic kind of way. He had to be nearly eight inches taller than she was and his arms looked so strong and protective.

"Elise Jenkins, I would like you to meet the detective in charge of the Carlson murder investigation, Mitch Burns."

Her eyes soaked up every detail of the detective's face as she reached her hand out to him. His brown hair had a subtle wave to it and was probably why he kept it so short. His eyes were a shade lighter than his hair and held tiny flecks of gold. His rugged complexion was softened by the smile she saw creeping across his face.

"Miss Jenkins, I'm sorry for being so short with you on the phone yesterday. I really appreciate the delay in your phone call until after I had a chance to come up for air. Unfortunately, I think I may have let all of the week's stress come out in my voice with you."

She was surprised at how glad she was to hear the detective's apology.

"I understand completely. I just hope you understand that I've got a job to do, too."

He nodded his head in what appeared to be a gesture of appreciation and then excused himself curtly, saying only that he had to head back to the station.

For some reason she was disappointed to see him go, yet couldn't ignore how on-off his personality seemed to be. Just when it seemed as if the ice was breaking, he froze up. Men.

"Thanks again, Chief." She walked through the parking lot, searching for more sources. The crowd had thinned quite a bit with many people waiting in their cars for the automobile procession to the cemetery. Elise placed her notebook inside her handbag and walked around the corner to the front of the church. The victim's best friend was sitting on the steps of the church as the pallbearers placed the casket into the hearse. The grief stricken young woman was curled up in an almost fetal position with her head on her knees.

"Maureen, right?" Elise smiled gently as the young woman lifted her tear-streaked face. "My name is Elise Jenkins, and I just started work as a reporter for the Ocean Point Weekly."

The girl nodded without uttering a word.

"I just wanted to tell you how sorry I am at your loss. My best friend, Celia, died when we were in high school and it was one of the most painful things I have ever been through. So, I understand some of what you are going through right now, and I'm sorry."

"What happened to her?"

"She died of cancer," Elise said quietly, her voice breaking as she spoke. "I know that the circumstances are like night and day, but I know how lost you must feel right now."

"The hardest part of this is that Susie was *told* that something bad was going to happen..."

The girl wiped at fresh tears that threatened to spill over her cheeks, as Elise was suddenly struck with the enormity of what she had just heard.

"What do you mean she was *told* something bad was going to happen? And by *whom*?"

She stared at the woman sitting in front of her, waited for some sort of explanation that would make sense. But as she waited, she noticed that the girl's eyes were beginning to glaze over. If Elise didn't back off she might not ever find out what the girl had meant.

"I can see that you have been through enough today so I won't keep you. But I would like to do a story about Susie so our readers can get a glimpse at the daughter her parents lost and the friend you lost as well," Elise said. She quickly pulled a business card out of her purse and jotted down her home number on the back. "If you want to talk, please call. Maybe you can help me put a face with the name everyone is talking about right now."

Without realizing what she was doing, Elise gave the girl a quick hug.

"I would like that, Elise, thanks." The girl rose to her feet and tilted her head in the direction of the hearse. "It looks as if they are ready to head on out to the cemetery now. Gotta go."

Elise watched as the young woman descended the steps of the church. Her exhaustion and grief were evident as she walked slowly past the black car that carried her friend's body. The sound of the woman's sobs filled Elise's ears as she reluctantly turned and headed back to the office.

# 4

## 3:30 p.m.
## Sunday, June 13

Beads of perspiration covered Elise's arms as she stepped off the beach and onto the road. Three hours of sunbathing had left her in dire need of a shower and a cool drink.

The tiny beach cottages along Dunes Road were starting to fill up with vacationers. A minivan with boogie boards strapped to the roof was parked in front of Elise's favorite cottage. Unlike many of the other rental properties surrounding it, the owners of this cottage were fastidious about its exterior. Because grass was too hard to maintain in a beach community, most yards were made up of tan colored landscaping rocks and very little else. But this particular house had a brick walkway and an inviting porch swing hanging beside the door. Flowering bushes and a mailbox shaped like a sand pail completed the look. She couldn't imagine a more special place for a kid to spend their summer.

She smiled at the little girl that happily ran out the front door and over to her dad who was filling his arms with suitcases. The look of anticipation for their vacation week wasn't hard to miss on either of their faces.

Vacations were something she was going to make a priority when she got married and had kids. Celia's mom always used to say "the families who play together, stay together" and Elise believed it. Hanging out at Celia's house in high school was the best. Everyone was so positive and upbeat. And loving. It had been a wonderful refuge from her home where negativity and criticism were the norm.

At the next block, Elise turned south. This road was primarily made up of well-kept duplexes and small apartment complexes. When she reached her building, she stopped to hose the sand off of her feet. The cold water felt good against her sweaty legs. But a shower would feel better.

She climbed the single flight of stairs to her door and stopped. Locating her key was going to be a nightmare. The bag she had grabbed on the way to the beach was way too small for all of the paraphernalia she had shoved into it. A bigger beach bag was in order for her first paycheck.

She reached in her bag and felt around. Book, towel, cassette player, suntan lotion...greasy key.

She grasped the small metal object at the bottom of the bag and pulled it out. Yup. It was greasy. And pink.

"Great," she mumbled, wiping her hand on the towel. "I guess my key won't be getting a sunburn anytime soon."

She turned the key in the lock and pushed the heavy door open, the sound of a ringing phone greeting her. She tossed her beach bag and sunglasses onto the floor and ran into the kitchen.

"Hello?"

"Elise?"

"Yes?"

"This is Maureen O'Reilly. We spoke the other day at Susie's funeral."

Elise's heart began to pound. The victim's friend was actually calling.

"Hi, Maureen," Elise said carefully, willing her voice to sound as relaxed as possible. "How are you feeling?"

"Not too good. I miss Susie so much. Then today, I started thinking. You know, about helping to tell everyone about the kind of person she was and what a great friend she was, and...," the woman's voice trailed off briefly. "I think I would like to talk to you."

"That would be great, Maureen. Do you want to come by the office tomorrow?"

"I was kind of hoping that maybe we could talk today." The woman was silent for a moment. When she spoke again, her voice sounded hesitant, yet hopeful. "If you aren't too busy."

Elise looked quickly at her reflection in the mirror over the couch. Her skin was red and blotchy from spending the past three hours in the sun. Her hair was matted with sweat and she looked anything but professional in a bikini top and ratty workout shorts.

But she knew that this might be her only shot at finding out what Maureen had meant when she said that Susie had been told something bad was going to happen to her.

"I've been at the beach all day and I'm not terribly presentable at the moment," Elise said honestly. "But if you can give me about 30 minutes, I would love to have you join me for a light dinner. I made a pasta salad this morning and there is plenty for two."

Elise could almost hear Maureen's smile over the phone. "I could use a little company, so that sounds great. Thanks, Elise."

After giving the woman directions, Elise hung up the phone and headed for the shower. The tiny granules of sand that seemed to cover every inch of her body were starting to make her itch.

The cool shower did wonders for removing leftover sand, but did little to dispel the tension in her shoulders. Would she uncover something today that might help shed some light on the case?

"Not if you don't relax," Elise chided herself. In the brief conversation she had with Maureen on Friday, she learned one thing for sure. The woman was going to clam up if Elise came across as being aggressive or too inquisitive.

She turned off the water and stepped onto the fuzzy bathmat. She knew she had to appear calm if she was going to learn anything interesting. She wrapped a large towel around her body and headed straight for her dresser. After careful consideration, she decided to simply wear a pair of tan shorts with a turquoise crew neck top.

Elise studied her face in the mirror. A quick dab of mascara to accentuate her blue eyes, and some clear lip-gloss certainly helped to improve the image she had seen looking back at her twenty minutes earlier. She pulled her wavy, shoulder-length hair up into a ponytail and secured it with a scrunchy. It would have to do.

She still had a few minutes to make a pitcher of lemonade before picking up the beach bag and sunglasses she had tossed on the floor when she came home.

A soft knock at the door changed that plan.

"So much for the lemonade," she whispered as she grabbed the bag and sunglasses and shoved them into the coat closet.

When she opened the door Elise found herself face to face with the woman she had met outside St. Theresa's a few days earlier. But she looked different somehow. Older. The sadness she was enduring over the death of her best friend was evident in the vacant look of her eyes and the black shadows that encircled them.

"Hi, Maureen, come on in."

The woman stepped inside, obviously unsure of herself.

"I was just about to make a pitcher of lemonade. Would you like some?" Elise offered.

"That sounds good."

Elise watched for a moment as the woman shyly looked at a few of the photographs Elise had mounted in a collage on the wall. She walked over to her and pointed at the photograph in the center. "That girl was my best friend, Celia. The one I told you about."

"She died of cancer, right?" Maureen asked, studying the picture. "She was very pretty."

"She was even more beautiful on the inside," Elise said. "It has been four years since Celia died and I still miss her every day."

Maureen nodded as she wiped at a tear that escaped down her cheek.

"I'll go make that lemonade now. Make yourself comfortable and I'll be right back."

There was no doubt that she had made a connection with Maureen. They had both lost a dear friend. That loss put them on a level field, and Elise no longer felt like a reporter with a subject. She only hoped that Maureen felt the same.

"Here you go," Elise said, handing Maureen a tall glass.

"Thanks."

After some initial awkwardness, Elise could sense that Maureen actually welcomed the chance to talk about Susie.

"Do you mind if I take some notes?" Elise asked gently.

The words seemed to spill out of Maureen's mouth as she nodded in agreement.

"It is so hard for me to think that my best friend isn't here anymore. We spent virtually every day together since we were six years old. We played dolls, rode our bikes, teased our brothers, shared our diaries with each other, went to college together, and even double dated from time to time," Maureen said as her voice cracked. "She had been extra happy lately because she'd gotten a great job with an accounting firm, and she had just moved into her own place."

Elise wrote rapidly.

"Madame Mariah had told her that all these wonderful paths would be opening for her. And it was all coming true," Maureen continued.

"Who's Madame Mariah?"

"Oh, she is one of the fortune-tellers on the boardwalk. Susie absolutely loved the excitement of hearing about her future. I get weirded out by that stuff, but she loved it."

"How many times did she go?" Elise asked with growing interest.

"I would say probably a couple of times a summer for the past few years. The last reading she had done before the boardwalk closed for winter had promised that she would find a well-paying job that would enable her to live some of her fondest dreams."

"Like getting her own place?"

"Exactly. And finding a boyfriend. She had been asked out several times by a fellow accountant in her office and she seemed to think he was a pretty nice guy. She and this guy dated a few times, but it never really amounted to much. And that's why she went back to have her palm read on Monday evening," Maureen continued.

Elise stopped writing.

"Susie had a palm reading just before she was murdered?"

"Yes."

"What was she told?"

"That's the wild part. Madame Mariah told her that she should be very cautious because a tragedy was about to happen," Maureen said breathlessly. "I had been waiting for her outside the fortune teller's booth and when she came out she was white as a ghost."

Elise leaned forward in her chair, waited for Maureen to continue. She couldn't even imagine what *she* would have done if she were the one warned of tragedy. Would she have laughed it off or run home and locked her door?

"Then what happened?"

"Susie dropped me off at my parents' house before going to her own place. And that's the last time I ever saw her." Maureen's shoulders shook softly as she began to sob.

"Did you tell the police all of this?" Elise asked quickly.

"Yeah. I told both Detective Burns and Chief Maynard," Maureen said as she tried to regain her composure. "Detective Burns seemed to listen to me, but the chief called it pure coincidence and dismissed it completely. Detective Burns even asked me if we had seen anyone we knew on the boardwalk that night and I told him that there were tons of people we knew. You see, Monday night is a popular night at the boardwalk for us locals. For whatever reason that's the one night each week that the summer tourists seem to stay in their condos and beach houses. So that's when we all like to go."

"Who did you see?"

"We saw people from St. Theresa's, old classmates from high school, Chief Maynard and his wife, the new mayor and his kids and some goof I dated for about two weeks one summer."

Elise wrote as quickly as she could to keep up with everything Maureen was saying. The girl seemed to be reliving Monday evening in her mind.

"Elise, do you think that Madame Mariah was actually trying to warn Susie that her life was in danger? Do you think that she could really know that?"

It was a good thing that Maureen's question seemed to be rhetorical, because the same question was burning inside Elise.

# 5

## 9:30 a.m.
## Monday, June 14

Elise flipped on the light switch in the windowless conference room and blinked at the sudden brightness from the fluorescent overhead light. The table was clear except for a copy of Sunday's paper spread out in front of a chair at the head of the table. Sam's chair, no doubt.

She walked across the room and set her notepad and pen down beside Sam's spot. She had ten minutes to gather her thoughts before everyone came in for the weekly staff meeting.

Last week she had felt uneasy, acutely aware of the fact that she was a novice compared to her coworkers. Although Sam had done his best to include her in the group's brainstorming session, she had little to contribute that first day and everyone knew it.

But today was different. The interview with Maureen yesterday had given Elise some very unique angles to explore in the Carlson murder investigation. Angles that would surely make her a contributing player at the table that morning.

She looked quickly at the list she had made at breakfast, bullet points of things she wanted to talk about. When the murder first happened, Elise couldn't help but feel she was at a disadvantage being an out-of-towner. Less contacts and familiarity with the way things worked in Ocean Point. But now that she'd had more time to think, the fact that she wasn't a native may actually play in her favor. She didn't have to take everything and everyone as a given.

"Hey 'Lise."

She looked up from her list and saw Dean Waters eyeing her curiously from the doorway. She pushed her notepad away, smiled at the photographer and patted the table top across from where she sat.

"Hi, Dean. Did you have a good weekend?"

"Yup. It was so bloody warm out that I busted open my windows and cranked the tunes. Don't think my neighbor was real pleased about it but there's not much the old hag *does* like so I've quit trying."

That did it. Her shoulders started heaving, and she clamped a hand over her mouth to stifle the laugh that echoed through the room. Dean was quite a character. And his most endearing aspect was the sincere clueless-ness he seemed to possess as to why people found him so amusing.

She tried to reply with something equally funny but ended up laughing again instead. It was hard to believe that someone as wild as Dean could be the genius he was with a camera. If she had seen him walking down the street in one of his infamous concert t-shirts with his long, unruly hair, she would have pegged him for a junky, not a photographer. But he could capture a person's thoughts almost as clearly as their outward appearance in virtually every shot he took.

"And here comes the queen herself..." Elise followed Dean's gaze to the conference room door and saw Karen Smith approaching. Next to Sam, Karen was the most seasoned staff member at the paper and made sure to let Elise know that when they had been introduced last week. Sam often referred to her as the "prima donna of the print world," and it was a title she seemed to bask in. "Shall we stand in respect?"

Elise dropped her gaze into her lap and bit her lip over the urge to laugh at Dean once again. He was going to get her in trouble one of these days.

"Good morning, Elise. Good morning, Dean," Karen said as she strode over to a chair and sat down.

"Goooooooood morning, Mrs. Smith!"

The scowl the society reporter flashed in Dean's direction was unmistakable and made Elise want to laugh even more. She was grateful when Tom Miller finally arrived and took Dean's attention off of Karen, enabling Elise to slow her breathing.

Tom was a pretty squared-away, easy-going guy. Not much Dean could stir up with him. His quiet nature endeared him to everyone on staff. And his sports writing had won the paper a number of awards over the past several years. The kind of awards Elise hoped to receive one day for her own news and feature writing.

"Okay, everyone, let's get started." Sam strode into the room and sat down at the head of the table. He looked around at the faces of his staff members and smiled quickly. "First off, I want to commend everyone on yet another outstanding paper yesterday. We had some tough material to cover with the Susie Carlson murder and you all handled it like the professionals you are."

He smiled and nodded his head in the direction of Elise and Dean.

"Elise, your coverage of the funeral was outstanding. Dean, you caught some great shots this week on both a serious and lighthearted note."

Elise tried hard to keep her smile under control, but Sam's praise got the best of her. She could feel her cheeks redden and hoped no one noticed.

Suddenly, the sound of an emergency siren escaped from Dean's mouth. "Look Pa, 'Lise is turning beet red. Quick, get the fire hose."

The room erupted in laughter as Tom made a sound of squirting water and Sam pretended to put on a fire hat.

Note to self, Elise thought as she watched the guys try to outdo each other's antics. Never, ever, sit across from Dean again.

She was thrilled when Sam finally cleared his throat and brought the room under control. "So, what are we working on this week?"

Tom took the ball and gave a brief rundown of the sporting events that were happening around town.

"The summer leagues are going strong for the little leaguers so I've got lots to cover there. I've also heard that Paul O'Neil is going to be vacationing here next week and that will be a neat story."

She wanted to ask who Paul O'Neil was but waited, not eager to draw unwanted attention for the second time that morning. With any luck, the questioning look Elise saw on Karen's face would result in an answer.

"Is Paul still playing for the Yankees?" Karen asked.

"No. He's retired now." Tom pulled out a sheet of paper from the back of his notepad and held it up for everyone to see. "Don't forget that the annual Family Fun Fest at St. Theresa's is this Saturday night. There'll be a celebrity volleyball match this year that should be pretty cool. It's gonna pit some of the town's head honchos against each other. Great photo ops for you, Dean."

"Thanks, Tom. How about you, Karen?" Sam shifted in his seat and took a sip from his coffee mug.

"I'll be covering a lot of the behind the scenes action in preparation for the festival as well as the silent auction and pie making contests during the actual event." Karen paused dramatically as she turned over the notes on the table in front of her before continuing.

"I'll also be starting some preliminary work on one of my profiles for later this month."

"Who's the subject?" Dean asked.

"Kevin Maynard."

"Maybe if you're really nice he'll show you all his medals and guns," the photographer whispered in a sensual voice.

Elise couldn't help it. She laughed out loud again. Karen's dirty look did little to help.

"Now, children," Sam teased. "Anyway, that sounds good, Karen. It's about time we got to know the police chief a little better. Now, Dean, I want you to shoot the devil out of that festival because I'm picturing a two page spread just for that."

"Gotcha. I'm also going to step up my tourist pictures now that the little buggers are starting to swarm all over town again. Fly swatter anyone?"

Sam just shook his head in amusement and moved on to Elise. "How about you, hon?"

The smile Sam flashed in her direction was all the encouragement she needed. She had kept her interview with Maureen to herself long enough.

"I had the most interesting talk with Maureen O'Reilly yesterday afternoon in my apartment. She was Susie Carlson's best friend," Elise said slowly, aware of the excitement in her voice. "She told me that Susie really loved having her fortune told by those ladies up on the boardwalk and, in fact, had just had her palm read the evening she was murdered."

"So much for the fortune-teller's ability, huh?" Dean said sarcastically.

"But that's just it, Dean. Maureen said that Susie was very upset when she came out after her palm reading because the woman had warned her of tragedy."

The room grew eerily quiet except for the sound of the clock ticking on the wall. Elise could feel the eyes of everyone in the room staring at her. Nervously, she flipped to the page in her notepad that contained her list of suggestions for stories.

"I was thinking that it would be kind of neat to do a feature story on the fortune tellers who set up camp on the boardwalk each summer.  Kind of an expose' about who they are and why people gravitate to them."

"Sounds like an interesting angle.  Go ahead and run with it," Sam said.  He pushed back his chair and stood up, an obvious signal that their staff meeting was coming to a close.  "It might be the first and last time we ever do a story on the fortune tellers if Johnson and Associates has anything to say about it."

"Why's that?" Elise asked.

"Because that's the portion of the pier they are hoping to level for their luxury condos."

# 6

## 5:30 p.m.
## Monday, June 14

*"C'mon, Cindy, it's* gonna be so cool. Don't you want to know if you and Bobby are gonna get hitched one day?"

If there was one trait she was glad she had missed when genes were being passed out, it was the one that made a person incredibly annoying...the one her cousin had gotten in spades.

"Sure I want to know, but these kind of places give me the willies." Cindy looked through the open doorway at the empty folding chairs and strange lighting. Was it possible for a place to be any creepier? She shivered.

"You need to loosen up, girl," Barbara said, propelling her into Madame Mariah's parlor. She plunked her money down and then reached into Cindy's purse for another ten-dollar bill.

"Remind me again why I asked you to visit me this year." She pulled her purse away from the overeager hands of her mother's favorite niece and shot her a glare.

"Because you have the time of your life every time I come to see you and you can't deny it." Barbara pursed her lips and blew a thin, pink bubble that expanded from her mouth. It grew and grew until she finally popped it with her teeth and sucked it back in. "Besides, without me, your life is nothing but school, work, an occasional movie with Bobby, and *endless* church functions with your parents."

Before she could come back with a clever retort, the fortune teller known as Madame Mariah pointed at Barbara and motioned her to follow with a long bony finger.

A feeling of overwhelming fear enveloped Cindy and she reached for Barbara's arm to stop her. But her cousin simply flashed a wicked smile and ducked behind the red curtain that separated the waiting area from the back room where fortunes were told.

Five minutes later, Barbara was back, beaming like a tree filled with Christmas lights.

"Well...?" Cindy asked nervously.

"My life is golden. Now it's *your* turn."

She felt her cousin's hand shoving her forward. She didn't want to go behind that curtain. It was creepy. And she knew that she would fall for whatever the lady told her. Even though the intelligent side of her knew it was a crock.

"Would you like to do your reading with Tarot Cards or your palm?" Madame Mariah asked.

Cindy could feel her mouth drop open as she stared at the imposing woman with jet-black hair and black-as-night eyes. It was like every creepy movie she had ever watched with Barbara; the kind where Barbara stayed glued in front of the television set while she made a lengthy popcorn run to the kitchen. But this time the only escape would be out to the waiting room where Barbara was sitting. And, if she did that, she would never hear the end of it.

She took a deep breath and walked slowly toward the rickety looking chair the woman pointed to.

"Well?"

Cindy looked at the crystals hanging from the ceiling, the deck of cards to the side of the table, the dim floor lamp covered with a black cloth, and back to the woman's heavily lined face. She squared her shoulders nervously and finally spoke, though how the woman heard her was a mystery in itself. "Let's go with my palm, I guess."

When the fortune teller reached for her hand, Cindy could feel a shiver run through her body. She made a mental note to herself to ignore Barbara's nutty ideas in the future.

Within seconds the fortune teller was shifting nervously in her seat.

"What's wrong?"

"This line right here ends abruptly—a sign of tragedy," Madame Mariah said. "You must be very careful. You are in very grave danger."

Cindy shrieked and pulled her hand out of the fortune teller's grasp. She jumped out of her seat and pushed the red curtain aside as she headed for daylight out on the boardwalk.

"Hey, Cindy! Wait up!" Barbara said.

She couldn't wait. She had to get as far from that place as possible. Her feet pounded on the boardwalk as she ran toward the bright lights of the game booths that seemed so far away.

A tug on her sleeve brought her back into the moment. She stopped and began to tremble.

"Cindy, what happened in there?"

"That lunatic said I'm in danger." She could feel the tears spilling down her face but could do nothing to stop them. "I told you I didn't want to go in there!"

"C'mon, cuz. She's a crock and you know it. I just thought it would be something fun to do but I didn't mean for you to get so upset." Barbara's hands grabbed hold of Cindy's shoulders and tried to steady her, calm her. "Just blow her off and don't give it another thought."

"Blow her off? Don't give her another thought?" Cindy screamed. The sound of her own voice startled her. She saw questioning faces turn in her direction as she spoke. People she knew. She had to calm down. She bit the inside of her lip and lowered her voice. "You're right."

They walked down the pier towards the spinning wheel games that almost always seemed to have cute guys working them. Only this time Cindy couldn't concentrate on anything other then Madame Mariah's words.

"Whoa! Check him out. What a babe," Barbara said.

Cindy watched as her cousin made a beeline for the game featuring compact discs as the coveted prize. The girl reached into her pocket, extracted a quarter, and slapped it down on the space marked "friend." It was amazing how Barbara could find money for some things and not others.

The game operator pushed a button and the large wheel behind him began to spin, clicking as the pointed arrow hit each piece of metal along the exterior of the circle. The clicking grew fainter as Cindy's mind went back to the ominous things Madame Mariah had said to her. Was she really in danger?

"I won! I won!"

Her cousin's shriek broke through Cindy's thoughts and she realized the wheel had stopped spinning. The arrow was sitting precariously on "friend." At least one of them was going to have a good night. Cindy shivered inexplicably.

"I want that *N' Sync* CD right there, because that's my cousin's favorite group." Barbara took the plastic box from the game operator and planted a kiss on his surprised face.

"Here you go, Cindy. I'm sorry I dragged you into that fortune teller."

"No big deal."

Now if she could just convince herself of that.

9:00 p.m.

"Cindy, would you run down to the corner and get me a gallon of milk?"

She looked up at her mom and smiled. It was the opportunity she needed to take a breather from Barbara. And, judging by the expression in her mom's face, that had been her intention. As much as her mom loved Barbara, she wasn't blind to the many differences between the two girls.

"Sure, Mom."

Her mom's mouth formed a silent "ask" while her head moved in Barbara's direction. That was mom for you. Even though she was fairly certain Barbara wasn't going to move from her spot in front of the television, she wanted Cindy to be polite and invite her along.

Cindy took a deep breath and crossed her fingers behind her back for good measure. "Do you want to come, Barbara?"

"Nah, I want to take a shower so we can hit the beach first thing in the morning."

Barbara's answer was music to Cindy's ears. She loved her cousin to death but she'd had more than enough of her for one night.

She walked the four short blocks to the store, grateful for the quiet. The more she thought about it, the easier it was to discard the fortune teller's warnings. It was all a game and she knew it.

The convenience store wasn't busy at all when Cindy walked in, just a few sunburned tourists wandering around aimlessly looking for the suntan lotion they hadn't thought to buy sooner. She grabbed a gallon of milk from the refrigerator case and walked up to the register. The cashier was an elderly man who lived a few blocks from home.

"Hi, Mr. Webber, how are you tonight?"

"Doing great, Cindy. Say 'hi' to your folks for me, will you?"

She nodded her head and smiled. "I'll do that. Bye."

Once outside, she decided to take the beach back to her house rather than the road. The pounding surf had been a favorite sound of hers since she was a little girl. It always cleared her head and helped her to refocus.

When she reached the beach, Cindy leaned down and pulled off her shoes. The cold night sand felt great between her toes. She looked up at the star filled sky and instantly searched for the Little Dipper. Her second grade teacher had been the first to show her what the constellation looked like and she had been fascinated by it ever since.

That's when she heard it. The sound of a footstep behind her, muffled slightly by the sand. Before she could turn around and see who was there, she felt a terrible pain in the back of her head.

Cindy fell to the sand, unable to move or say anything. She could feel a sticky warmth trickle down her neck. She tried to focus, tried to see the face of the person who tugged at her index finger. But it was no use. Everything went black.

# 7

## 11:00 p.m.
## Monday, June 14

It was one of those nights when no matter what she did, she couldn't sleep. Warm milk didn't help. Soft music didn't help. Staring at the ceiling didn't help. There was just too much on her mind. The fortune teller connection to Susie Carlson was just too hard to let go and she was excited about the feature story she had pitched to Sam that morning.

Elise threw off her sheet and slipped out of bed. If she wasn't going to sleep, she might as well use the time to get some work done. She pulled on some sweatpants and a light jacket and grabbed her purse. The office wasn't that far away and the walk would do her some good.

She hoped that being in the newsroom would help get her thoughts down on paper so that she would be able to sleep. So many ideas were swirling around in her mind for her feature on the fortune tellers. But she had to pick an angle and she had to come up with the questions she would ask.

The dim light over the door to the building shed just enough light for her to locate the office key on her key chain and insert it into the lock.

She flipped the switch and blinked as the large fluorescent light turned on. They were great lights to work by when you were in a building with few windows, but they were torture on your eyes when you first turned them on. She rubbed her eyes briefly and went straight to her desk, rummaging through her top drawer for a brand new note pad.

Maureen had said Susie was warned of tragedy after a palm reading. How can a crease in someone's hand mean life or death? And how does someone even go about *becoming* a fortune teller? She jotted each question down as it popped into her head, not wanting to forget a single one when she finally came face to face with Madame Mariah.

A long, slow beep made her jump. Elise spun her chair around and searched the room with her eyes. The sound came from the police scanner in the corner of the room. She ran over to the machine and turned the volume up, listening carefully to the dispatcher's voice. A homicide. At the beach. The location of the body was just two blocks from the office! She grabbed her notebook and pen and ran for the door.

As she approached the beach, Elise could see that half the police department was already there, including Detective Mitch Burns. The officers scurried about, flashbulbs flashed, and the detective spoke into a recorder in his right hand. She wanted desperately to hear what he was saying, but she knew she had to stay out of their way and let them do their job.

She planted herself on an edge of the beach that was illuminated by a high-powered spotlight the police had set up. It was a great spot to be. Perfect light for writing and a great vantage point for watching the police conduct their investigation.

She was close enough to tell that there was indeed a body, but far enough away that she wouldn't be haunted by the vision. She quickly jotted down some initial observations about the scene.

She listened closely as Detective Burns ordered the department's photographer to get as many shots of the victim as possible. She noticed as he took charge of the men around him, giving each one a job to do. Even though she had only spoken to him twice, it was obvious to Elise that Detective Burns was under great pressure.

Suddenly, she saw him whirl around and stare at her.

"Miss Jenkins, this is an active crime scene and I must ask you to leave. Call the department tomorrow and I will give you a statement at that time."

"Detective, I want to do whatever I can to help you in your investigation, and I think our readers would like to know that their home town is the site of another murder," Elise said. She mustered up every ounce of courage she had and looked the man right in the eyes. "Can you at least tell me the victim's age?"

"She's a teenager. Look, Miss Jenkins, I don't have time for this right now. If you really insist on being here then you need to keep out of our way," he said firmly.

She nodded quietly and did as she was asked.  As intense as her job was right now, the detective's was harder.  In one week's time he had two horrific crimes thrown at him and nothing but endless questions from everyone in town.  She took a step backward, hoping to relieve some of his anxiety over her presence.

The smell of the salty sea permeated the air around them, rolling waves crashed again and again.  It was hard to imagine such a beautifully peaceful place could be the scene of something so disturbing.  Elise quickly jotted down a few more observations and then turned toward the road.

The lights from a car behind her caught her attention.  The station wagon screeched to a stop just a few yards from where she stood.  A couple in their early forties jumped out of the car and ran toward the beach, a teenage girl just steps behind them.  A police officer held them back as they approached the victim's body.

The woman screamed in terror.  "That's Cindy! That's my baby!"

Elise watched in horror as the man grabbed his wife and pulled her away from the gruesome scene.  What was left of the quiet night was shattered, the woman's screams growing louder and louder as reality sunk in.

She turned away, wanting to give the couple the privacy they so desperately needed.  But the girl who had gotten out of the car with them stood just a few feet from Elise, alone in her shock and grief.  She started over to her, hoping to offer the young girl a shoulder to cry on, but her legs wouldn't move.  She didn't know what to say.  Suddenly, the girl spoke in a low, raspy voice that was audible to no one but the two of them.

"Oh my God.  Madame Mariah was right!"

9:00 a.m.<br>Tuesday, June 15

Elise sat across from Sam's desk with huge black circles under her eyes.  She had managed to get only two hours of sleep last night.  She knew her voice sounded almost wooden as she gave her boss a quick update on the murder investigation and the comment she had overheard from the victim's cousin.

Sam shook his head slowly as he listened to every word Elise told him.

"That fortune teller story you mentioned at the staff meeting yesterday...get on it right away."
"Yes, sir."

# 8

## 10:30 a.m.
## Tuesday, June 15

He *carefully removed* the crime scene pictures from the large manila envelope on his desk. The head shots, the wound shots, the full-body shots, the location shots. Each picture a chilling reminder of the fact that two young women were dead, two families altered for the rest of their lives.

Mitch looked at the picture of his parents sitting on the right hand corner of his desk. His father had been so proud to wear the uniform, so in love with Mitch's mother. It was hard sometimes to remember what it was like when they were both alive. He remembered all the baseball games his dad had missed when Mitch was a kid because an emergency call had come in at the last minute, sending him out the door and into his squad car. For so many years Mitch hadn't understood, seeing his dad's absence as a lack of interest. But as he'd gotten older and made his way through high school, he had finally realized what a hero his dad really was.

He shook his head quickly and forced his gaze back onto the photograph of last night's victim. Seventeen years old. A baby! And the look on her mother's face when she saw her daughter lying on the beach...

Mitch remembered the day the phone rang like it was yesterday. Dad had been shot while crossing the street to pick up his uniform at the dry cleaners. No suspect. No motive.

The funeral had been a blur; so many people had come to the church that a local news station had set up a big screen in the parking lot for the people who couldn't fit inside for the service. His mom had been so quiet through it all, doing her best to get Mitch through the whole ordeal.

But his mom was the one who needed help. As days turned into months and no suspect was ever charged in Dad's death, she became more and more withdrawn. Until one day she simply didn't wake up. Although there had been a fancy medical word that explained her death, Mitch knew it was a broken heart that killed his mom. His dad's killer had struck twice.

"Hell will freeze over before I let that happen to these families." His teeth clenched over the words, a sentence he needed to hear as much as he needed to say.

He simply couldn't let another family live life without answers. He picked through the pictures, taking mental notes as he looked at each one. There was a ton of work to do. The Medical Examiner's report on both victims had been similar. Each girl had died as a result of a sharp blow to the back of her head. The weapon used was a wooden object of some kind, evident by a small amount of splintered wood found inside the wounds.

He looked again at each picture closely, searching for any additional clues that might link the two homicides together. But the mountain of paperwork on his desk made it hard to spread everything out.

Mitch ran his hand across his eyes and through his hair. He needed to bring some semblance of order to the evidence that would enable him to look at everything closely, a way to go back and forth between each case with ease. He pressed the intercom button on the bottom of his desk phone and waited.

"Yes, detective?"

"Could you get your hands on a card table of some sort for me? I need a flat, open space to work on right now and my desk is trashed."

"Sure thing."

He had an idea that just might help him in his investigation. He gathered up all the personal information he had obtained on each victim and walked over to the empty chair across from his desk. A soft knock interrupted his thoughts.

One of the department's college interns opened the door and began setting up the card table in the spot Mitch indicated.

"Thanks. This is going to be a big help." He immediately began laying each photograph across the top of the card table. He considered the arrangement momentarily and quickly reorganized the items so as to have the body shots in one area, the scene photographs in another.

The next step was to tape the personal data onto the wall directly above the table. Satisfied with the layout for the time being, Mitch pulled up a chair and sat down. He turned on his recorder and started talking.

"Okay, let's start with the basics. We've got two females. One age 24, the other age 17. Both girls have grown up in Ocean Point. The first victim was killed in her apartment; the second victim was killed on the beach. Both murders happened in the late evening and both girls were struck with a blunt wooden object from behind."

He studied each photograph carefully, looking from one victim to the other as he tried to see any visual similarities that existed between the two.

"One blonde, one redhead. Very different build and size..."

His words trailed off as he leaned in closer for a better look at the full-body shots. Both girls had the index finger of their right hand extended when their body was discovered. Were they trying to provide a clue of some sort?

Maybe. But it struck Mitch that it was more likely that the finger had been positioned in that manner *after* death.

He looked closely at the scene directly in front of each victim's body. In the first murder, Susie Carlson was in her kitchen. The only thing in the path of her finger was the refrigerator.

He looked at the teenager's surroundings next. The only thing she could have been pointing at would have been the beach.

"Okay, great. I've got an appliance and a sandy beach. Outstanding clues you found there, Mitch. I can see why you were promoted to detective."

His Aunt Betty was always bugging him about the way he criticized himself out loud. But it was a habit. And this time she would have to agree that his ramblings made little sense.

He was chasing his tail. There were no two ways about it.

He pushed back his chair and wandered into the hallway. He grabbed a Diet Pepsi from the small fridge in the department's lounge area and started back towards his office. As he passed the chief's office, he looked in and saw Kevin Maynard sitting at his desk with his back to the door.

He knocked.

"Oh, hey there, Mitch. How's it going?" The chief pointed to the empty chair in front of his desk. "Any progress in the investigations yet?"

Mitch sat down. He had to share his frustration with someone, and Chief Maynard was as good as anybody.

"I really believe these two murders are connected. They just have to be. There are too many similarities for it to be a coincidence, but they aren't pointing me in any direction yet."

Pointing. It came back to the fingers again. It had to be significant. His mind trailed off momentarily as he thought again about the position of the index finger on each victim's right hand.

He realized the chief was speaking to him.

"We have got to get these murders solved as quickly as possible. I've gotten calls from just about every member of the council today and every one of them is afraid of what this is going to do to the tourist season," Chief Maynard said. "I haven't heard from Mayor Brown yet, but I am sure his call can't be far off. You know *he's* not going to be pleased with the scrutiny this town is receiving because of this."

Mitch rose to his feet and headed for the door. "I'll get back at it right now."

"One thing is for certain. My request for more manpower in the department should be a no-brainer for the council now, huh?" the chief said, a self-satisfied smile creeping across his face.

Mitch nodded distractedly and headed back to his office. He had decided to turn his attention away from the photographs momentarily and focus on the background information each victim's family had given about their daughter. He pressed the record button once again.

"The first victim was an alumnus of All Saints High School. The second victim had just completed her junior year there last week. Both girls were members of St. Theresa's Parish."

Father Leahy. Maybe a call to the priest would shed some light on something, anything. If nothing else, maybe he could offer up a word of wisdom or two for Mitch that would help him get through these investigations quickly so the families would at least *know*.

The buzzing of the intercom broke his train of thought. He wished the front desk would leave him alone for a while, let him get some work done. But, no such luck. He pressed the button on the phone. "I really can't be disturbed right now."

"An Elise Jenkins from the Ocean Point Weekly is on the phone and she said it was important that she talk to you."

It was a shame how he seemed to be in such a lousy mood every time she called. She was so pretty and everyone who had met her had nothing but nice things to say about her. And the way she had stepped away when the victim's parents had broken down last night...

"Okay, put her through."

"Detective Burns, I wanted to tell you about a comment I overheard from the victim's cousin last night that I thought you might be interested in."

He couldn't help but notice how her voice matched her sweet face.

"Shoot..."

"She said they had gone to a fortune teller up on the boardwalk early last evening and had their fortunes told."

Her words hit him like a ton of bricks. Another connection!

Not wanting to let on his excitement at the information, he calmly asked her for more details.

"The girl said that her cousin had been told that she was in danger. I found that to be most interesting in light of the fact that Susie Carlson had evidently been warned of the same type of thing just last week."

"How do you know that?" he snapped, furious that someone had leaked that bit of information.

"I'm a good reporter," she retorted.

There was no doubt about that.

"Anything else?" he asked.

"No, that's it for now," Elise said.

"Why did you call to tell me this instead of just running with it in the paper first?"

"Because I think we can accomplish more if we work together."

"We'll see," he responded. She really was a class act, he thought. "Thank you, Miss Jenkins."

After he returned the receiver to the phone's cradle, Mitch found himself feeling a measure of disappointment that the conversation was over. Maybe when this whole investigation was wrapped up he could get to know her a little bit better.

He turned back to the card table and wrote the words *fortune teller* in big red letters across his notepad.

He grabbed for the case file on his desk and looked up the phone number for the murdered teenager. When the girl's father answered the phone, Mitch identified himself and asked to speak with the cousin Elise had mentioned.

A few moments later, Mitch heard the phone being handed to someone else.

"This is Cindy's cousin, Barbara. How can I help you?" whispered the strained voice on the other end of the line.

"I understand that you and Cindy had your fortunes told on the boardwalk last night. Is that true?"

"Yes. I pretty much forced her to do it, even though she told me she didn't want to."

Mitch waited a few moments while the teenager worked to slow her speech and control the tears she was obviously choking back.

"Madame Mariah did a palm reading on Cindy and told her that she should be careful." He could hear her voice cracking over the words, her tone becoming more desperate. "And then we came back to Cindy's house and she went out for milk and then she got killed."

Good old Madame Mariah. He knew she was one of the more colorful psychics up on the boardwalk. Always worth a few laughs. Only, this time it wasn't funny.

"Now, Barbara, I need you to think carefully. Did you or Cindy see anybody that you knew while you were on the boardwalk last night?"

"I don't really know anybody here because I'm just visiting from Kentucky. But I remember Cindy waving to several different people when we first got there."

"Did she tell you who any of the people were?"

"She said one of them was a guy she worked with at the miniature golf course. Another was a lady who lives on the same street, a Mrs. Anderson, I think. Some cute guy she introduced me to...I think his name is Jacob Brown. He was there with his mom and dad."

He jotted down the people: co-worker, neighbor, Mayor Brown and his son...

"Anybody else?"

"I think she said the police chief was there, too. Yeah, she did. She said that he always reminds her of Nicolas Cage with a moustache."

Mitch smiled. Somehow he thought the chief would get a kick out of that description.

"Thanks, Barbara. You've been a big help."

He added Madame Mariah's name to his notes.

He knew that Johnson and Associates was working hard to win the approval of the town council to tear down the boardwalk's first pier, the same pier that was home to Madame Mariah's fortune telling business.

He pushed the red button on his recorder and spoke slowly, thinking his thoughts aloud. "Perhaps Madame Mariah could be trying to prove her importance by 'predicting' these tragedies and then somehow playing a part in carrying them out."

His thoughts started racing. Why would she want to be involved in something like this? Wouldn't it be obvious that crimes likes these would only serve to work in the developer's favor? Or could someone be trying to help the fortune teller's *removal* from the pier?

The last thought stuck. He couldn't ignore the fact that the first pier was made up primarily of fortune tellers and an occasional copycat game of chance.

Working on a hunch, Mitch pressed the intercom button.

"Yes, detective?"

"Could you get together a file on Johnson and Associates for me? Any and all information about them, their dealings with the town, past projects, anything like that?"

"I'll get right on it."

He shut the recorder off and glanced at the clock on his desk. 4:30 p.m. He had worked straight through lunch. He rubbed his forehead and reached for the bottle of Tylenol he kept in his upper right hand desk drawer. Empty.

Out of nowhere, he suddenly found himself replaying a part of his earlier conversation with the chief.

*"My request for manpower in the department should be a no-brainer for the council now..."*

Mitch could feel his mouth growing dry, his heart beginning to race as his thoughts turned in yet another direction.

He thumbed through his notes and stopped. Both of the victims had seen the chief on the boardwalk the night they were killed.

"C'mon, Mitch. The chief can't be that desperate for a larger police force," Mitch said, and then shut his mouth quickly when he realized he had spoken his thoughts aloud.

He could feel the chill running through his body. It couldn't be. It just couldn't.

Even so, he found himself thinking about the best time to come back to the office in order to examine another file. A file that he could never ask the intern to put together.

# 9

## 9:00 p.m.
### Wednesday, June 16

Elise climbed the short flight of steps from the beach to the boardwalk, eager to learn as much as she could about Madame Mariah. At the very least, their time together would provide essential information for her feature story on fortune tellers. But it was the best case scenario that made her heart race. Because maybe, just maybe, she would uncover some sort of clue about why two of the woman's clients had been murdered.

She stepped onto the boardwalk and stopped; her senses in overdrive. The smell of cheese steaks and calzones filled the air. Seagulls circled overhead, waiting to swoop down and catch a few crumbs. The pounding surf was a backdrop to the clicking of the game wheels and the friendly yet persistent banter of the vendors. This was the kind of place Celia's mom would have taken her family on vacation. A place with fun and excitement and wonderful memories-in-the-making. She wished Celia could be here now with her family, wished she could be anywhere, with anyone. But it wasn't meant to be. So she would enjoy it *for* Celia.

She looked around at the games and people. The pier was peppered with a variety of games, some chance and some skill. Spying a favorite game of hers, she crossed the pier.

"Three frogs for a buck or seven frogs for two bucks," said the heavyset man behind the counter. He had more tattoos on his arms than Elise had seen in a lifetime.

She handed him a dollar. He pulled three wet rubber frogs out from under the counter and handed them to her. She carefully folded the long, scrawny legs under the body of her first frog and positioned it on the platform in front of her. With careful precision, she slammed the mallet down onto the circular lever and watched as the rubber frog sailed through the air and splashed into the water.

She repositioned the catapult, loaded the second frog onto the platform and slammed the mallet down. This time her frog's head landed on the lily pad, its rubbery legs dangling in the water.

"Yes!" She shot her hands into the air and did a little dance where she stood.

"Gotta get it all the way in the lily pad, lady."

"Oh, come on," she protested. "Only his legs are in the water."

"That's two legs too many, lady."

One big whack later, Elise finally had a prize to show for her efforts. She selected a pink teddy bear with a cute face and tucked it under her arm.

"Nice shot, lady."

Elise glanced at her wristwatch quickly and froze. She had been so wrapped up in having fun that the whole reason for being there had temporarily escaped her mind. If she didn't pick up the pace, her visit with Madame Mariah might be in jeopardy and that was one interview she didn't want to have to reschedule.

She looked at the game attendant and patted the bear. "Thanks. It'll be a nice addition to my apartment. Hey, do you know where I can find Madame Mariah's place?"

"She's down there," the man said, pointing his tattooed finger in the direction Elise needed to go.

As she walked, Elise's eyes were drawn to the amusement rides illuminating the night with their bright, colorful lights. Loud music piped in through speakers added to the excitement that emanated from the crowd. Youngsters screamed in delight as they walked carefully across a moving floor on the open-faced fun house. Others screamed in terror as they emerged from a nearby haunted house. Teenagers lined up for the rides that made them sick to their stomachs and parents shelled out money for the costly tickets.

The first pier, where the fortune-tellers were located, was much quieter. If she didn't have work to do, this would have been an ideal spot to do some people watching.

There seemed to be people who knew exactly where they were going at this end of the boardwalk. Regulars, no doubt. And then there were others who hung around the booths trying to muster up the courage to consult the psychic inside.

She read the names over each doorway until she found the one she was looking for, Madame Mariah's House of Fortunes.

*Learn about your future from the Queen of Visions* read the neon sign that was fastened to the wall. She took a deep breath and stepped inside.

The waiting room was nothing like she had expected. But, then again, she really hadn't known what to expect. Astrological charts hung on the walls in an obvious attempt to cover the peeling paint beneath them. A variety of crystals dangled from the ceiling. Hushed voices could be heard from behind a red curtain, but other than that Elise was alone. She sat in a folding chair and waited.

Suddenly, a man parted the red curtain separating the waiting area from the back room and walked towards the front door. She knew the face but couldn't place him.

"Thanks again, Mariah. As always, I feel like you are clearing my path and pointing me in the right direction."

"My pleasure, Ben. I'll see you again."

"You can count on it." He grinned and walked out onto the boardwalk.

Elise watched the man leave and tried to put a name with the face. But she couldn't. She turned her gaze instead to the woman who stood just inside the parted curtain. The woman was everything Elise had imagined and more. Her jet black hair pulled into a tight bun, large gold hoop earrings, and her long, flowing dress all added to the mystical aura the fortune teller exuded.

Elise looked the woman over once more from toe to head, stopping on the unreadable eyes that stared back at her. She shifted in her seat and then rose, surprised by the apprehension she suddenly felt.

"I'm Elise Jenkins with the Ocean Point Weekly." She extended her hand to the fortune teller.

"I know who you are."

"Really? How do you..." Elise could feel her mouth drop open, her heart skip a beat. Maybe the lady really was psychic.

"I know all. Plus, I saw your picture in the paper when you started your job there."

Elise laughed. She was glad to see that the woman had a sense of humor. Hopefully it would make her job a little easier.

"I'm here because of the two girls who were murdered in Ocean Point," Elise said. The woman's face darkened instantly. "I was told that both girls had consulted you for a fortune the night they were killed."

"That is right."

"Evidently you had warned both girls of tragedy."

47

"That is also right."

Realizing the woman was not going to be very forthcoming, Elise got straight to the point.

"Can you tell me what you saw when you read their palms? What you believe may have happened?"

"I did a palm reading on each of those poor girls." Madame Mariah continued, her words spoken in a slow, deliberate fashion. "Their Life Line ended abruptly."

"Their Life Line?"

"Your hand contains three main lines. The top line is your Heart Line and it can tell about your romantic life in the past, present and future. The second line is your Head Line and it can tell about your career, your goals, that kind of thing. The bottom line is your Life Line."

Elise jotted down everything the woman was saying.

"Anything else?" she prodded.

"They were punished for their visit."

Elise looked up from her notes and stared at the woman.

"What do you mean by that?"

"I mean just what I said," the woman said gravely. "Now, I must go."

Confused, Elise thanked the woman and turned towards the door. The psychic's words rang in her ears. She looked around wildly for something to prolong the conversation, a way to get Madame Mariah to explain her cryptic words. Her gaze stopped on a strange assortment of scorch marks around the door, the kind of thing Elise would expect to see after a fire.

"What happened here?" Elise pointed at the marks, hoping and praying the woman would say something.

Madame Mariah walked over to the doorway and placed her hands, palms down, on the singed wall. Elise watched in fascination as the woman closed her eyes and began to speak.

"Evil and greedy forces are trying to get rid of me."

"Are you saying that someone tried to set this place on fire to get you off the boardwalk?" Elise asked, her voice rising in pitch.

"The fire department said it was caused by a cigarette that had been carelessly disposed of, but I know that none of my clients that day were smokers."

"Do you think it was deliberate?"

"Evil and greedy forces will do whatever it takes to accomplish a goal," Madame Mariah said. The woman walked toward the curtained room and turned. "Good night, Elise."

# IO

## 4:00 a.m.
## Thursday, June 17

He felt like a traitor. Chief Maynard had been nothing but supportive and understanding since the day he stepped into the top spot at the department. He always seemed to understand Mitch's crusade to solve everything, regardless of how small or trivial. And he lent a listening ear on more than one occasion when Mitch threw a tantrum over the latest perp to get off with a slap on the wrist from the county judge.

Yet here he was in the middle of the night, getting ready to go through his boss's personal files to see if something might point to him as a killer. Mitch shoved his hand against the file drawer, shutting what he had just opened. He couldn't do it. There was no way he was going to turn on the chief like this.

But what if the chief *did* do it? Could he really turn his back on the possibility because Maynard was a nice guy? Mitch ran his hand across his eyes and over his hair. Would he have wanted the cops to overlook a suspect in his dad's killing?

No.

His hand shook as he turned the key in the lock. This time he didn't stop the drawer as it rolled open. Instead, he ran his fingertips across the names of his fellow officers, their personnel records bulging with references, psychological evaluations and background checks.

He wondered what his dad would say if he were still alive, what he'd think of his son investigating the department's chief. But he knew the answer. Dad had been a firm believer in loyalty through the ranks. He would be ashamed of his son and Mitch knew it.

But Mom would have wanted the truth, no matter where that led. It was the not knowing that had been the hardest for her.

Mitch sucked in a deep breath of air and reached for the file belonging to his commanding officer, Kevin Maynard. For several long minutes he stared at the file, toying with the idea of putting it back and disregarding his fears. But he couldn't.

He shut the drawer and locked the cabinet. Once inside his private office, he locked the door for added privacy. He flipped the folder open.

> *Kevin Maynard. Former military. Served a tour in Vietnam in 1970 at the age of 18. Retired from active duty after 20 years. Followed his father's example and entered civilian law enforcement in Sumter, a small town about 30 miles away. Worked his way up from patrolman, to detective, to captain. Was next in line to become that department's chief. But left and came to Ocean Point instead.*

"Now, why would he do that? Why would he walk away from his pension?" Mitch said aloud. He flipped to the application the chief had filled out when he applied to the Ocean Point Department.

According to what the chief had written, he had felt compelled to leave his former department because of a difference of opinion regarding a missing persons investigation.

Mitch searched each subsequent piece of paper in the chief's file for particulars on the difference of opinion, but there were none. In fact, the chief's file seemed unusually thin considering his position in the department.

"That's odd. I wonder why the town council didn't pursue this." He shook his head as he realized he was speaking out loud again. Using a recorder so much had given him a nasty habit that he needed to break.

Mitch glanced at the clock and realized Chief Maynard would be arriving shortly for his morning run. He pushed back his chair, closed the file, and headed back to the records room. It wasn't until the chief's file was safely back in the locked cabinet that his breathing slowed to normal for the first time in hours.

The missing persons case the chief had referred to on his application had to have occurred during his last year with the Sumter P.D. And it had to be a pretty major disagreement to make a person walk away when he was next in line for the top job. Mitch needed answers and he knew just where he could find them.

His lunch break would be a perfect time to visit the Sumter Public Library.

*11:30 a.m.*

It *was becoming* more and more difficult to read the stack of papers in front of him over the loud gurgling from his stomach. The slice of toast he had eaten eight hours ago wasn't cutting it anymore.

"Here you go, sir. Here's one more issue about that terrible ordeal."

Mitch looked up long enough to smile gratefully at the elderly librarian. She had attached herself to him from the moment he requested information on a missing person story from two years earlier.

Maynard was quoted in several stories from that time period while he was a captain with the Sumter Police Department. His quotes all concerned leads and clues. All very professional. All very innocent.

Mitch flipped carelessly through the next five or six issues in front of him, feeling foolish for driving all the way to Sumter for something that was apparently nothing.

He turned another page and stopped.

*Psychic Consulted in Disappearance of Local Boy.*

Intrigued by the headline, Mitch read the article. Three paragraphs down he found it. Kevin Maynard was quoted as saying "Psychics and fortune tellers are all whackos. They are simply trying to make a fast buck at the expense of innocent people."

Mitch was surprised by the strong words, particularly to a member of the press.

Several issues later his boss was made to eat those words when the missing youngster was found—safe and sound—exactly where the psychic had told them to look.

"That had to be humiliating."

"What was that, hon?" the librarian asked.

He was doing it again. He really needed to work on keeping his thoughts inside his head instead of on the tip of his tongue for everyone to hear.

"It must have been a real shock when that psychic was able to nail down the location of the missing boy." Mitch pointed to the article he was reading.

"Oh, it was! It was just amazing! That little boy's parents were so thrilled." The woman sat down in a chair next to Mitch and continued, obviously thrilled to be able to rehash a story she would never forget. "The whole town was excited. Except, maybe, for a gentleman that was working for the police department at that time. He thought it was ludicrous to give a psychic the time of day. But then, a few days later, it was that very psychic who solved the case."

"Do you remember the name of the officer?" Mitch asked. He didn't know why, but he needed confirmation of what he had just read. Someone to validate a motive for murder taking shape in his mind. A motive for *two* murders.

"May, May something. Anyway, he was ridiculed by many a people in this town for his skepticism. I imagine he hates the mention of a psychic these days."

Mitch quickly stacked the newspaper issues on the table in front of him and stood. He squeezed the woman's hand gently.

"Thank you. You have been an enormous help."

# II

## 1:00 p.m.
## Thursday, June 17

*Everything she could* possibly want to know about Ocean Point was right there at her fingertips. Pages and pages of the town's history were neatly bound in large volumes and arranged on the shelves by decade.

"I see you found the morgue."

Elise spun around. Dean stood in the doorway, a camera bag slung over his arm.

"The morgue?"

"You just can't learn everything in those journalism colleges, can you? This room. It's called the morgue. Because it holds all the old copies that get thrown into a book and forgotten." He set his bag on the ground and walked into the room. He ran his finger across a dusty maroon cover on the 1950's shelf and held it up to her. "I think Sam forgot to pay the housekeeper."

She narrowed her eyes at Dean, looked him over from head to toe.

"If the photography thing falls through, you could pass for a Swedish maid," she teased.

He tried to hold it back, but she saw it. The corner of his mouth twitched in an upward movement.

It felt good to goof around with Dean. It helped ease some of the troubling thoughts that had been plaguing her mind since she left Madame Mariah's place last night. The burn marks around the psychic's doorway were hard to ignore on their own, and when you threw in her eerie response, it was enough to cause insomnia.

"You look tired, missy," Dean said, looking her over. "You okay?"

"Yeah, I'm okay. I just didn't sleep real well last night."

"Take it from me. Warm beer works every time."

She crinkled her nose at the thought. "I'll keep that in mind, thanks."

He picked up his camera bag once again and walked back to the door. "I've got a shoot to do, so I'm outta here. Don't work too hard."

Elise was almost sad to see him go. His presence had kept her from the task at hand, helped lighten her mood. But she needed to get moving.

There was only one person she could come up with who would have a reason for wanting Madame Mariah off the pier. A fire seemed a bit extreme, but it was possible.

She located the book with last year's papers and pulled it off the shelf. Opening it, she flipped to the beginning of last summer. She skimmed the back issues looking for the first article she could find regarding Johnson and Associates' proposed luxury condominium complex.

She found it in an issue from mid June.

*According to Daniel Johnson, president of Johnson and Associates, a new luxury condominium complex would enable Ocean Point to accommodate seventy additional families each week during the tourist season, bringing more revenue to the town and its businesses.*

*The proposed condominium complex would require demolition of the first pier of the boardwalk, a pier that has not been a huge revenue maker in recent years.*

*"The vast majority of Ocean Point's tourists are attracted to the various games, food booths and thrill rides that are found only on the second pier," Johnson said. "And it doesn't take much research to realize that the majority of police calls to the boardwalk are to those establishments on the first pier."*

The article went on to quote council members as well as tourists about their opinion on the proposed project.

One council member said that Ocean Point was doing just fine in the number of vacationers it could accommodate each summer. Another said that demolition of the first pier would be an easy way to get rid of the "less than desirable" people such places attract. A vacationer from northern New Jersey felt the boardwalk as a whole was sentimental to her family...fortune tellers and all.

Elise continued to turn the pages that chronicled the tourist season in Ocean Point last summer looking for anything that might catch her eye. And then she saw it. It was mentioned briefly in a blurb on the second page of a July paper.

> *A small fire on the boardwalk was quickly extinguished last night by a fast thinking passerby. Joseph Copetti, of Brooklyn, was walking down the boardwalk with a friend when he saw flames climbing the outer wall of Madame Mariah's House of Fortunes.*
>
> *"I still had my beach blanket from earlier in the day, so I ran down to the beach and dipped it in the water and then ran back onto the boardwalk with it," Copetti said. "I smacked the wall over and over with the wet blanket until I got the flames out while my friend Vinnie went and called the fire department."*
>
> *Madame Mariah's, which was closed during the incident, sustained only cosmetic damage and no one was injured. A spokesperson for the Ocean Point Fire Department blamed a smoldering cigarette just under the doorway for the fire.*

Madame Mariah had been certain none of her customers that day smoked. So how could a lit cigarette get inside and go unnoticed from the time the woman closed until the fire was spotted almost four hours later?

Maybe Madame Mariah was right. And, if she was, it sure seemed like Johnson and Associates had a motive for trying to burn her out.

She closed the book and returned it to the shelf. Maybe Sam could shed some light on the whole matter. She wandered out into the hallway and headed towards his office.

Sam was obviously deep in thought. He was pushing buttons on his calculator and writing numbers down in a large notepad. Tomorrow was deadline day for Sunday's paper. It was time for Sam to calculate the amount of space advertising would have to fill and how much space editorial would get.

Not wanting to interrupt his concentration, Elise stood in the doorway and studied him. The fluorescent light fixture above his desk cast a bright shiny spot on his head. She found his baldness to be endearing. It fit him perfectly.

During her interview for the job, Sam told her he had always wanted to be a fiction writer but had to hold down a day job in order to pay the bills. Working in the newspaper business had given him a way to get paid for writing. After 18 years with the paper, he had taken over as editor—a position he still held 12 years later.

Elise watched as Sam turned the calculator off and stretched his arms above his head. Mid yawn, he finally noticed her.

"Oh, sorry. What can I do for you, Elise?"

"I was just looking through last summer's papers in the morgue."

"Find something interesting?"

"I was wondering if anyone had ever considered the fire at Madame Mariah's last year to be suspicious."

"It went through my mind at the time, but the fire department was certain a cigarette was to blame."

"I spoke with the fortune teller last night and she is convinced no one had been smoking in her place that day. In fact, her exact quote was, 'evil and greedy forces are trying to get rid of me.'"

"In this town, that woman is considered to be a very highly paid entertainer and nothing more," Sam said. "The police chief, in particular, is one who just won't give much credence to her ramblings."

"I noticed that talk of the condo complex seemed to die out by summer's end last year, yet it's back again this summer. What do you think that's about?" she asked him.

"I think Daniel Johnson is hoping that a new mayor may help his endeavor."

"What kind of guy is this Daniel Johnson?" Elise questioned. She noticed Sam's mouth tighten, his eyes narrow.

"I don't like him at all. There's something sneaky about that guy. But I just can't seem to put my finger on what it is about him that bothers me so much."

"Try," she prodded.

"Well, first of all he's from New York. And when you're from Jersey, that's reason enough."

She laughed. She was beginning to realize that the whole New York/New Jersey thing was a lot like Missouri and Illinois. In reality there was no difference between people in either location, but to hear the residents of each state talk...it was two totally different cultures and each one thought theirs was superior.

"Secondly, he has questionable business tactics in my opinion."

"For instance..."

"One of the council members was dead set against the idea of another condo complex in town because he felt we had as many tourists as we could handle. So, Johnson did a little research and discovered this same council member wasn't too crazy about the kind of clientele the first pier can attract sometimes."

"And he played it, right?"

"You got it. He played it hard. And sure enough, he managed to sway the guy's vote."

Elise nodded as she considered her boss's words.

"Do you think it's possible he could have had something to do with that fire last year, maybe hoping to get rid of the first pier in a more expedient manner?" she asked.

"Entirely possible, but it would be virtually impossible to prove at this point."

She weighed his words in her mind as she leaned against the doorframe of his office. If a fire wasn't enough to get the fortune tellers off the pier, what about a murder or two?

"Do you think he could have a hand in these murders, as another way to get rid of the fortune tellers?" Elise watched Sam's face as he considered her question, saw his fingers tighten into a fist on his desk.

"I certainly hope not," he said quietly.

"I was thinking that maybe I could schedule an interview with Daniel Johnson to discuss his proposal and do an updated version of last year's story," Elise said. She had always prided herself on her ability to pick up a person's true essence. Maybe it would come in handy with the developer.

"Sounds good, but why don't you meet him over lunch where there are other people around," Sam suggested.

"He makes you that nervous?"

"It's probably ludicrous, but after 30 years in this business you develop a kind of sixth sense about people. And mine is in full blown radar mode where that creep is concerned."

"Okay, boss. I'll arrange a lunch meeting for next week." She playfully saluted him in an effort to relieve the tension that hung in the air.

She watched in amusement as he raised his right hand to his forehead in response.

# I2

## 11:00 a.m.
## Friday, June 18

*She stopped counting* when she reached one hundred. Each car followed slowly behind the one in front, the headlights hard to see in the brilliant sunshine of the summer day. The sadness that hung over the town was suffocating.

Elise forced herself to move away from the window. The funeral was over and another family was shattered. She had a ton of work to do and looking out the window was not going to get it done any faster.

It was deadline day and she had finally finished the feature story she had been working on for most of the week. Wanting to see how it looked in the actual paper, she headed back to the small composing room located in the back of the building.

The draft tables were strewn with pages and pages of what would eventually be Sunday's edition of the Ocean Point Weekly. The advertisements had already been pasted onto the pages. The large blank spaces were a less than subtle reminder of all the work the rest of them had to do before 5 p.m.

Dean's weekly photo page was already laid out. Her coworker was definitely blessed with a talent for capturing memorable images.

She smiled at the look of uncertainty on the toddler's face as he navigated the difficult task of walking on sand for the very first time. The picture of the teenagers playing touch football on the beach was a great shot and the large photograph of a little girl licking an ice cream cone on the boardwalk was simply precious.

She scanned several more pictures before settling on a small shot of the new mayor leaving church last Sunday. His warm smile and wave to the crowd was exactly what you would expect from a politician. But his wave needed work. With his thumb and pinky tucked downward, he looked like a boy scout preparing to recite his sacred oath.

She knew she was wasting time. Those blank spots in the paper weren't going to get filled by themselves. But she just wanted to take a peek at how her story was laid out. Then she'd get back to business.

The front page of the lifestyle section brought an end to her search. The fortune teller story looked great. And she was very pleased to see that Dean had managed to catch the mystical aura that was as much a part of Madame Mariah as her dark hair and penetrating eyes. Even the side story on the various techniques used by the psychics held its own.

All she needed now was a teaser on the front page of the paper inviting readers to turn to the lifestyle section to read it. Maybe a quote from the new mayor regarding the undeniable popularity of the fortune tellers during the summer months would fit the bill. It was worth a shot. And besides, she needed to call him about another story anyway.

Elise glanced at her watch. The mayor should be back in his office by now even if he had attended Cindy's funeral. She peeked out the window once more. The funeral procession was long gone and, from what she could see, things were getting back to normal on the streets of Ocean Point. As normal as it could with a murderer on the loose.

But it felt wrong. Wrong to be sitting on a beach or shopping in a store or eating an ice cream cone when two families were facing life without their daughters. Elise looked down at the pale yellow sundress she wore. The tiny sprig of flowers that dotted the bodice section had caught her eye in a small dress shop on Ocean Boulevard just after she moved to town. She had felt so pretty and upbeat when she finally put it on that morning, but now it felt wrong, too. Disrespectful somehow.

Elise sighed and turned away from the window. She couldn't do anything to change what had happened. But maybe her work could keep it from happening again. She walked over to her phone and placed a call to the town hall. After identifying herself and requesting a few minutes of the mayor's time, she was quickly put through to his line.

"Hello, Elise. Are you looking forward to the festival at St. Theresa's tomorrow?"

"I almost forgot about that with everything else going on around here, but, yes, it should be fun."

"So, what can I do for you today?" His voice was strong and self-assured.

"I have a few things actually, but I'll try to make it as quick as possible. I was hoping to do a story on your first month in office. How it has compared to what you envisioned, the direction you would like to see Ocean Point move in, that kind of thing."

"Sounds great, fire away."

She flipped her notepad to a clean sheet of paper and prepared to write.

"First up. Can you tell me what some of your immediate goals are for the remainder of the summer tourist season?"

"I want to make sure the wholesomeness of our town is portrayed clearly to the people who choose to vacation here each year," he said. "I want our rental property owners to make a concerted effort to rent their cottages and condos to families only. By doing this, we can better avoid many of the problems other beach towns have faced when they have allowed overzealous college kids to vacation there without proper supervision."

She stopped writing for a moment as she pondered what the mayor said.

"Wouldn't those property owners have to be careful about discrimination if they put a policy like that into place?" she questioned.

"Certainly. But, if our town as a whole caters to the family crowd in everything we do and offer we won't be attractive to the wrong sorts of people."

"What do you see as ways for the town to cater to the family?"

"We need to really push the miniature golf establishments, the family style restaurants and the innocent fun of the amusement pier."

She decided to take advantage of the subject to get his opinion on the fortune tellers. A quote from him would be perfect for her teaser on the front page.

"What about the boardwalk fortune tellers? Do you think *they* attract the wrong sort of people?"

"Fortune tellers are imposters, plain and simple. They are exactly the kind of people who attract everything we *don't* want in our town."

His strong words surprised her, but not as much as the passion with which they were said. There was no doubt about it; Mayor Brown had no use for fortune tellers or anyone else who threatened the vision he had for Ocean Point. Maybe a teaser from him wasn't such a great idea after all.

"I'm preparing to move my ailing parents into my home in Ocean Point, and I want them to know they are in a town of high morals and values," he continued.

She stopped writing for a moment and fiddled with her pen. It was hard to know just how to take the mayor. One minute he seemed rather narrow minded, the next he seemed to be a man with a really big heart. How could she really fault him for wanting Ocean Point to be a safe place to live?

"That's quite an undertaking. You're a newly appointed mayor in a town that has been suddenly plagued by two violent crimes; you're an involved father with two teenage sons; you're heavily involved in various organizations affiliated with St. Theresa's; and now you're taking on the role of caretaker for two elderly parents. That's a lot on one person's plate."

"Well, Elise, it's like the Bible says: 'Honor thy father and mother.' It's my duty."

She jotted down his last remark and stopped. He would be a perfect subject for a shadowing story.

"Would it be possible for me to come and spend a few hours shadowing you one day next week?" She looked at her calendar as she waited for his reply.

"Absolutely. Is Tuesday good for you?"

"I have a lunch appointment with Daniel Johnson that day so I'm afraid our time together would be too limited. Would Wednesday or Thursday be a possibility?"

"Thursday at 9 a.m. would be fine."

"Wonderful. Thank you so much for your time this afternoon, Mayor Brown."

"You're welcome, Elise. I'll be seeing you at St. Theresa's tomorrow for the festival and again at Mass on Sunday, right?"

Just what she needed. Another parent.

# 13

## 6:00 p.m.
## Saturday, June 19

If the lasagna tasted as good as it smelled Elise would be in good shape. She hadn't been eating well lately and she knew it. Peanut butter sandwiches and leftover pasta salad were getting a little old. And her computer made a rotten dinner companion.

But tonight she was going to enjoy every bite of her dinner. And although she didn't know more than a handful of people, it was quite obvious that St. Theresa's 20th Annual Family Fun Fest was the place to be that night.

There was enough food on the buffet tables to feed an army and she was eager to sample as many of the delicious looking items as possible. The enormous basket of rolls in front of her looked heavenly and without thinking she found herself reaching for two.

"Are you sure you can fit two rolls into that little body?"

She could feel her face begin to redden. Not wanting to be impolite, Elise simply smiled at the elderly man next to her in the dinner line. It was just the kind of comment her grandfather would have made, a good laugh for him but mortifying for everyone around him. She skipped the next few items on the table in an effort to put as much distance between herself and the eyes of the self appointed food patrol behind her.

But, unfortunately, as Elise neared the end of the table, she came face to face with the biggest threat to her willpower. Dessert. Like the mother ship calling her home, she slyly reached for a frosted brownie that was just too enticing to ignore.

Finally, armed with a plastic fork and knife, she set off in the direction of the eating area located in the large yellow party tent just a few hundred yards away. Numerous tables filled the temporary dining room, virtually all of them playing host to animated discussions between people who obviously knew each other well.

Elise deliberately chose a small table near the back of the tent so as not to draw too much attention to the fact that she was alone. She couldn't help but feel a twinge of sadness as her mind traveled back to those lonely pre-Celia lunches in the high school cafeteria. If only she had "come into her own" a few years earlier, she may have actually enjoyed her teenage years.

"Hey, 'lise, want some company?"

She was thrilled to see Dean standing beside her table. He set his heaping plate down next to hers without waiting for a reply.

"Looks like some good grub doesn't it?" he continued, as he shoved a roll in his mouth.

She wondered what the townspeople thought of the photographer. He just didn't match the image of the small, religious community. The long blonde hair was disheveled on a good day and his sense of humor was biting at times.

"Have you gotten any good pictures yet?"

"Yeah, I just got a great shot of Feather Leahy in the dunking booth."

The sound of her own laughter was just the medicine she needed to chase away the doldrums that had threatened to ruin the beautiful evening just a few moments earlier. She reached for the brownie.

"I noticed the volleyball game is going to start in about fifteen minutes. Are you playing?"

"No way. Too much testosterone in one place for me, thank you very much. But Sam is playing and that should make for some comical shots all on its own." Dean shoved a large cookie into his mouth.

"Who else is playing?"

"I think they're playing four man teams. Sam's team has him, the fire chief, the bakery owner and some other dude I don't know too well," Dean answered between swallows. "The other team has Mayor Brown, Chief Maynard, Mitch Burns and a very wet Father Leahy."

"Want to make a wager?" she asked playfully.

"I take Sam's team. What's at stake?"

"Loser sits in the dunking booth, winner gets three shots."

"You're on."

They gathered the garbage from their table and tossed it in the trash can. Since Dean seemed to have the lay of the land, she let him lead the way. When they reached the volleyball court he put on his

65

professional demeanor and began taking shots of the players as they prepared for battle. Elise found a spot on the sidelines.

As her team took their positions, she stood up and cheered. The curious look from Detective Burns made her tone it down a bit. She still wasn't sure how to read the detective, but she wasn't going to give him any false ideas about the motivation behind her cheering. Finger crossing would have to work this time.

Three sets later she was painfully aware of the fact that she should have stuck with the cheering. The finger crossing hadn't been terribly successful.

"Ready to get wet?"

Dean's smug smile was a lesson she would not soon forget. Betting was bad. Very, very bad.

"Something came up and I gotta go..."

Dean grabbed her arm and propelled her to the now vacant dunking booth.

Like townsfolk at a stoning, people seemed to appear out of nowhere as she scooted onto the wooden plank across the top of the tank. She silently berated herself for thinking a wager like this would be fun.

Fortunately for Elise, it didn't take long to realize why Dean had pursued photography rather than athletics. Two balls down and she was bone dry.

"Come on, Dean. Can't hit the target?" She smiled wickedly at the photographer and stuck out her tongue. It was kind of fun sitting in the booth. It was a great place to sit and watch people.

Suddenly, Mitch Burns stepped out of the crowd surrounding the booth and whispered something in Dean's ear. She was horrified to see the long haired rat hand over the final ball to the well built detective.

Before she could remind Dean about the terms of their bet she felt the plank give way beneath her.

# 14

## 8:00 p.m.
## Monday, June 21

She had planned on saving Mia's Chinese Restaurant for a treat after payday, but she couldn't wait any longer. It had been a humiliating day and she wanted nothing more then to drown her sorrows in a cardboard box of fried rice.

Elise stopped in front of the restaurant and inhaled slowly. A hint of soy sauce hung in the air and wafted outside through an open front window. She closed her eyes briefly and tried to relax. Tomorrow had to be better. And in the meantime, she didn't have to go home to an empty apartment and cook. But even as she tried to visualize the spare ribs and pepper steak she planned to order, all she could see was Dean Water's head on a plate surrounded by rice.

It had all started with the 8 X 10 glossy print she found taped to her computer monitor when she arrived at work. The picture was a close-up of her face as she emerged from the bone chilling water in the dunking booth Saturday night. The sheer misery she had felt as she popped out of the water was captured in all its glory for the entire office to see. And if that hadn't been embarrassing enough, the round of applause she received from her coworkers surely was.

Once the obnoxious clapping had finally subsided, Sam had laughed and said that it served Elise right for betting against him. And all she kept thinking was how much she wanted to make Dean suffer.

Sacrificing Dean for use in a new Chinese dish might work. And at the very least it might save a few unsuspecting cats.

Elise chuckled softly under her breath at the thought and pushed open the door of the restaurant. The woman behind the front counter had to be Mia. She looked exactly as Elise's coworkers had described. Now if only their description of the food could be as accurate.

"Welcome. What I get for you?"

Elise reached for the folded blue menu perched on the corner of the counter and opened it. Her favorite Chinese fare was listed right on top.

"I would love a small order of spare ribs, a large pepper steak with white rice and a bottle of water, please."

"That be eight dollar."

She pulled out her wallet and handed the woman her last twenty dollar bill. Friday needed to come fast or this might very well be the last thing she ate for the rest of the week. She thanked Mia, collected her change and walked toward the back of the dining room to wait until her number was called.

Elise was glad to see only one other table was occupied. All she wanted to do was sit down, relax and enjoy her dinner. But then she realized who the other person was and froze.

Mitch Burns.

"Glad to see you've dried off, Miss Jenkins." A slightly crooked smile crept across the detective's face, irritating her all the more.

"No thanks to you," she shot back.

"Look, I'm sorry about the other night. It just seemed as if every time we've spoken to each other I've been abrupt with you. I just wanted to try and correct the impression I think you have of me."

"By dunking me? I think you should have stuck with the first impression," Elise said. She set her handbag on a clean table and sat down.

"Oh, come on. Accept a guy's apology and give me another shot. If you join me for dinner I promise not to get you wet." He jumped up and pulled out the chair beside his.

Not wanting to seem like a spoilsport, Elise moved her handbag to his table and sat down.

"I've never seen you here before," he said as he sat back down in his own seat. "Would you like one of my egg rolls while you wait for your food?"

"No thanks. Mine should be ready any minute now." It was obvious the detective was trying to make an effort to be friendly. "I've been wanting to try this place out for a while and tonight seemed like as good a night as any."

"You won't be sorry. Mia makes the best Chinese food around."

She looked around at the pale yellow walls dotted with personal photographs of a different time and place. Her gaze moved across each and every picture before turning again to her spot at the table. And Mitch.

"Numba 2!"

Mitch jumped to his feet before she could move. "I'll get it for you. It's the least I can do after nearly drowning you the other night."

She was glad she had decided to come here. And in some ways she was glad the detective had chosen to eat at Mia's tonight, too. It was nice to have someone to talk to over dinner and the fact that he was cute didn't hurt. She smiled at him as he returned to the table with her food.

"It looks great."

"Wait till you taste it."

He was right. It had to be the best Chinese food she had ever eaten. She took another bite and smiled.

"I wish I hadn't waited so long to come here." She wiped her mouth with a paper napkin.

"Why did you?"

"I haven't gotten my first paycheck from the paper yet and I'm kind of living on limited cash right now. I've been eating at my apartment or brown bagging it at the office every night. It gets a little lonely sometimes."

If only she could delete her own dialogue the way she could on the computer. She really didn't mean to tell him she felt lonely sometimes. She barely knew the guy.

Fortunately, he didn't seem to notice.

"I noticed in your write-up in the paper that you graduated from the University of Missouri," he said. "What made you look for a job here?"

"I don't know. I guess I just feel like being out on my own and this looked like a neat place to be. Did you grow up around here?"

"Northern Jersey, actually. But I went to college about 50 miles from here on a baseball scholarship."

"*That* explains your first shot the other night," she said, shaking her head in feigned disgust.

"Sorry."

She was surprised by his seemingly genuine apology.

"Anyway, I ended up blowing my elbow out and had to give up the whole baseball thing. So that's when I decided to go the police route instead," he continued.

"How long have you been in Ocean Point?"

"Four years. Worked my way up from patrolman. The early stuff wasn't terribly interesting, but I love the investigative stuff."

"It seems like it would be an exciting job."

"Not as exciting as it's been the past two weeks. These murders are putting me through my paces alright."

"I know exactly what you mean. I thought my first few stories would be fluff stuff just to get me into the swing of things." She took a small bite of spare rib, a sip of water. "But I ended up getting broken in with a murder, followed by another a week later."

"It's the weirdest thing. Until two weeks ago, this was a pretty quiet town—almost boring at times," Mitch said. "The biggest news around here for the past few months has been the mayoral election. Then Bam! Now I'm working 15 hour days trying to solve two murder cases."

"Any leads yet?" she asked, knowing the answer to her question before he even uttered a reply.

"Can't discuss that, sorry."

"Can't blame a girl for trying."

She took another sip of water and thought for a moment. Maybe he would be a good person to bounce her questions off of.

"Can I run a thought past you about the murders?" she asked.

"Shoot."

"I know from my research that Daniel Johnson has been trying to win approval from town council to build luxury condos where the first pier now stands. Don't you think it is odd that both victims consulted a fortune teller on that same pier just hours before their death?"

"Yeah, I do think it's weird. But following that same train of thought, why would someone want to kill two innocent women to get rid of a fortune teller?"

"I know it sounds crazy. But, maybe, if everyone begins to turn against the fortune tellers, approval to tear down that particular section of the boardwalk would be easier to get," she said then stopped. He probably thought she sounded so amateurish. "Oh, forget it. You don't need a junior detective clogging your thoughts, do you?"

"Or maybe the fortune teller is trying to show everyone how invaluable her service is."

"True." Elise was surprised at how seriously he seemed to be taking her thoughts. She studied him for a few moments as he pushed his food around the plate with his fork. He seemed so troubled and distracted all of a sudden. And it was her fault. The poor guy probably needed a break even more than she did and here she was talking about work.

She decided to change the subject.

"Do you like living in Ocean Point?"

"I love it. Right now my whole life is work, but I love the beach and the clean air and the laid back pace of everything."

She nodded and smiled. "The weather has been so perfect the past few weekends that I've gotten to enjoy the beach quite a bit."

"I can tell. You look like a bronze goddess," he said.

She could feel her cheeks blushing.

"Have you been to the boardwalk yet? It's a lot of fun."

"Once. I interviewed Madame Mariah for an article I did in yesterday's paper."

"I read that. Nice job," he said with what seemed to be genuine sincerity. She blushed again. "I would love to hear about some of the stuff you two talked about, but I'm in dire need of a break from work right now. So I'll hold off on asking about it 'til the next time."

Next time? She could feel the shyness of old creeping in as she sensed Mitch trying to find the nerve to ask her something. She saw his hands fiddle with the fork, heard him clear his throat a few times before he finally spoke again.

"Would you want to walk over to the boardwalk with me and get some fresh air?" he asked. "We could ride a few rides or just play some games."

She was surprised by the nervousness he showed as he waited for her answer. She found it to be endearing.

"Sure. Why not?"


9:30 p.m.

He knew he was beaming. Aunt Betty would be so proud.

He cast a sideways glance at the girl next to him. Elise Jenkins was beautiful. Her wavy brown hair was pulled up on one

71

side of her face, accentuating her cheekbones. And when she smiled, her gorgeous blue eyes lit up. There was something so sweet and honest about her. He found himself hoping the next few hours would go very slowly.

"Here we are."

The sound of her voice pulled him out of his thoughts. He knew he better stop staring or she would think he was a nutcase.

"Great. What do you want to do first?" he asked. He gently put his hand to her back and guided her up the wooden steps.

"What's your favorite game?"

"That would have to be any of the games where I get to throw. I have a pretty good arm," he said.

"I know...I was at the receiving end of that arm on Saturday, remember?"

The tension he felt over what to say and how to act seemed to evaporate instantly. She was being playful and that helped.

"Let me win you a stuffed animal to make it up to you."

He reached for Elise's hand and pulled her over to a booth that featured a back wall covered with dishes.

"Three balls for a buck," the gray bearded man said. "Break the dish and you win."

The vendor pointed to a collection of enormous stuffed dogs sitting in the back corner of the booth.

"That's got to be a really hard game, Mitch, or they would never have prizes this big for breaking one dish..."

"That's what he wins if he breaks three plates, lady. This is what he gets if he breaks just one plate."

The man held up a key chain.

"Just keep your eyes on the fourth plate from the right," Mitch said as he pulled his right arm back and launched the ball. The plate shattered into a million pieces. "Now watch the plate to the right of where that one was."

Again, he pulled his arm back and threw the ball. Again he destroyed the plate.

With his hand firmly grasped around the third and final ball, Mitch threw with precision aim and broke the third plate.

The look of amazement on Elise's face was worth it. She was in awe and he loved it.

He pointed to a big brown dog wrapped in plastic and waited for the vendor to bring it over.

"I guess the big rides are out now, huh?" he said sheepishly, as he took the dog and balanced it on his shoulders.

Her laugh made his heart melt.

"We could just walk the whole length of the boardwalk and enjoy the sights," she suggested.

"Sounds great to me."

As they walked along the boardwalk he was amazed at how many familiar faces he saw.

"I've lived here less than four weeks and I'm recognizing people left and right," Elise said.

"I was just thinking the same thing. Just since we left the game booth I've seen the town clerk and her boyfriend, a guy from church, and look...there's Mayor Brown and his family." He pointed toward the entrance to the first pier.

"Maureen said Monday was a big night for the locals to visit the boardwalk."

"Who's Maureen?" He touched his hand to the small of Elise's back and guided her around a puddle of melted ice cream.

"Maureen O'Reilly. Susie Carlson's best friend."

"I never really noticed before, but now that you mentioned it, I guess she's right."

The glass-covered counter to their right caught his attention and he reached out for Elise's arm.

"Have you ever tried salt water taffy?" He cocked his head in the direction of the brightly wrapped candy sorted into piles.

"No. Is it good?"

"It's the best. Next to my Aunt Betty's pies, salt water taffy is my favorite dessert."

"Okay, I'm sold. Let me treat since you won me that adorable stuffed dog," Elise said, smiling.

"No way. The dog was my way of apologizing for dunking you. The taffy is my way of saying welcome to Ocean Point."

He pointed to the red colored taffy at the end of the display case and pulled his wallet from his back pocket.

"I'll take half a pound of that."

Two minutes later, he opened the white cardboard box and offered Elise a piece. A man's hand reached inside.

"Thanks, Mitch. Don't mind if I do."

It was the chief.

"Hey, chief." Everything he had read at the Sumter Library hit him at that exact moment. Was he ever going to be able to look at his boss again without being suspicious? He forced himself to look at the chief and act as if nothing had changed. But it was hard. "You remember, Elise Jenkins, don't you?"

"I sure do. It's nice to see you again, Elise."

Mitch watched as Elise smiled and shook his boss's hand. She really was a class act. Very polite. Full of energy. And he didn't want to waste another moment of their time together talking to the chief.

After exchanging a few pleasantries he politely excused them so they could continue their walk. Alone.

He was glad when he finally had her all to himself again. He reached into the box and pulled out a piece of taffy.

"Try it, it's the best."

Her fingers brushed against his as she took the candy. He watched her long, slender hands unwrap the taffy and hold it up to her mouth.

"Mmmmmm." Her eyes widened, the boardwalk lights reflecting back at him. "And you say your Aunt Betty's pies are better than this?"

He laughed. "Believe it or not, yes."

"Are you close to your aunt?"

"She took me in when my mom passed away."

He felt Elise's eyes on him, searching.

"How old were you?"

"Sixteen."

"What about your dad?"

"He was killed about six months before Mom died."

"Mitch, I'm so sorry." He looked down at her worried eyes and smiled gently. He didn't want her to feel uncomfortable or sad. He didn't. In fact, he couldn't remember a time when he felt more at peace then he did at that very moment walking beside Elise.

"So what's the big food in Missouri?"

"Food?"

"Your version of salt water taffy."

"Toasted Ravioli."

"Sounds good." He wished he could reach out and hold her hand but he didn't want to scare her off. Instead, he slid his hand into the front pocket of his jeans. "Do you miss Missouri?"

"No."

He was surprised by how glad he was to hear that. He was completely at ease with her and it felt great. In some ways it was like they had known each other for years, yet at the same time he was very aware of the fact he didn't want to blow it by saying or doing anything stupid.

Before he knew it they were just a few feet from Madame Mariah's place. A familiar face emerged from the psychic's doorway.

"I saw him there the other night when I was waiting to talk to Madame Mariah," Elise said under her breath. "Evidently he's a regular."

Mitch stared at the man as he passed them, trying to place the face. The shadows cast by the moon made it hard to see the man's features clearly. Whoever he was, it was obvious he was upset. "He sure doesn't look too thrilled with his fortune tonight."

"I think he goes to St. Theresa's," Elise said as though reading Mitch's mind. "Madame Mariah called him Ben."

"That's it! I knew I knew him from somewhere. That's Ben Naismith from my men's group at church. He's relatively new, but from what I've seen so far he's a good guy."

They continued to walk.

"It looks like we're about to run out of boardwalk, Mitch."

Her words broke the momentary silence between them and he stopped, looked into her questioning eyes and wished he could add three more piers just so he could spend more time walking beside her.

"Want to walk back on the beach?"

"I'd love to. But do you mind if I take my shoes off? I love the feel of the sand on my feet." Her hand reached out for his arm as she gently kicked each foot forward. She reached down and picked up her sandals.

It felt so good to walk along the beach and forget about all the chaos of the past two weeks. The pounding surf was hypnotic in its ability to drown out unnecessary thoughts. The only thing he wanted to concentrate on right now was getting to know Elise. Unfortunately, it was getting late and they both had to work in the morning.

"I had a really great time tonight, Elise." He stopped and turned toward her.

"I did, too. I've almost forgiven you for dunking me," she said with a sweet laugh.

The sound of the surf faded as he reached out and gently pushed a wind blown curl from Elise's forehead. She was so nice and so pretty and he didn't want the night to end yet.

He wanted so desperately to lean over and kiss her, but just as he was building up the guts to do it his cell phone rang. Mitch shrugged his shoulders apologetically and pulled the flip phone from his back pocket.

"Detective Burns."

He covered his opposite ear to drown out the crashing waves.

"Looks like we've got another homicide, Mitch."

"Where?"

"In the parking lot off Sandpiper Lane."

"I'll be there in twenty."

He cursed softly under his breath as he shut the phone and put it back into his pocket.

"What's wrong, Mitch?"

"Another body. This time in a parking lot just a few blocks from here," he said quickly. "I'll walk you back to your place and then I've got to go."

"I should go, too."

He touched her shoulder gently. "Elise, let me check this out. I'll tell you what I can first thing in the morning."

**11:30 p.m.**

He *saw the* body as soon as he pulled into the parking lot twenty minutes later. He slammed on the brakes and jumped out of his car.

"What do we have?" he asked the officer nearest the body.

"Male victim, early thirties. Looks as if he was hit with a wooden object of some sort."

Mitch grabbed a flashlight from his glove compartment and shone it on the lifeless body lying on the ground in front of him.

He knew who it was as soon as he saw the clothing. It was Ben Naismith!

# 15

## 9:00 a.m.
## Tuesday, June 22

"Got those pictures for you, Mitch."

He reached for the folder the department photographer held and flipped it open to the first shot of Ben Naismith's body.

"Three murders in two weeks, who'd have thunk it?" Pete said, looking over Mitch's shoulder at the photograph.

"Not me. Hell, Pete, I wasn't prepared for the first one, let alone two more. But maybe these pictures will help somehow. Thanks for getting them to me so quickly." He pulled the second picture out of the folder and leaned over it, examining every detail he could find.

"Hey, Pete..." Mitch looked up from the pictures and realized the photographer had left. It wasn't a surprise, though; he didn't seem to be aware of much of anything this morning except for the fact that he was swimming in a shark tank and didn't know how to get out.

Mitch sat down at his desk and rested his head in his hands. He had never felt as incredibly overwhelmed as this. What he needed was a plan.

He pulled out each picture Pete had left and studied them closely. Like the other two victims before him, Ben's body was face down. A blow to the back of the head was the cause of death according to the Medical Examiner's preliminary report, and the man's right index finger was pointed outward just like the first two victims.

"Every one of these victims has been killed on a Monday night, after spending time at the boardwalk," Mitch said aloud. "Could there be some crazed person vacationing here who has selected his victims after seeing them on the boardwalk?"

He reached for his recorder with disgust and hit the red button.

"Elise pointed out that Monday night is a big night for locals on the boardwalk. So maybe it's not a tourist at all. Maybe the killer is someone local."

"But why these three people? What do they have in common?"

His eyes went immediately to the profiles of the first two victims which were still taped to his wall over the card table. He opened his top drawer and pulled out the new sketch he had compiled during the night.

"Okay. All three victims are residents of Ocean Point, two of the victims were alumni of All Saints High School and one was still attending school there. We've got two females and one male, so it's doubtful that the suspect is avenging a particular sex.

"And all three victims had consulted Madame Mariah prior to their demise..."

A loud knock at the door interrupted him. He pressed stop.

"Come in." He looked up as the door swung open, his boss's face set with rigid lines.

"Mitch, what do we have on this latest victim?"

"I'm reviewing all three cases right now, sir." He waved his hand in the direction of the crime scene photographs and individual profiles spread out in front of him. "The most interesting link is the fact that all three victims had consulted a particular fortune-teller the evening they were killed. Both of the female victims were reportedly warned of tragedy by the psychic, but I'm not sure what the latest victim was told. If I had to take a guess, I would say it was a similar fate based on the way he looked when he walked out of Madame Mariah's place last night."

"Those psychics are all crazy. I wouldn't put it past any of them to cause an event and then make a 'prediction' to validate their so called abilities," the chief said, his face darkening with anger. "I want you to question that fortune teller immediately."

"Yes, sir."

"And if this doesn't prove to the town council that we are understaffed, I don't know what will."

He didn't know why, but he felt as if he should applaud when his boss finished speaking. Maybe it was everything he had read at the Sumter Library that made Mitch so quick to judge his boss's every word and facial expression. But it was more than that. He just couldn't shake the feeling that he was getting his own first hand proof that something wasn't right where these murders and his boss were concerned.

When the chief left, Mitch reached for a clean sheet of paper and made two separate columns. He denoted the first column as possible motive, and the second column as possible suspect. As he considered the crime scene photographs and personal profiles in front of him, he quickly wrote down several scenarios.

"The fortune teller could be involved directly, or via someone else, as a way to prove to people in Ocean Point that her services are far more than just entertainment." He stopped for a moment, his pen poised above the paper as he considered the next possibility. "We've got a developer who has been pushing for demolition of Madame Mariah's pier so he can build a luxury condo complex that will bring him big money. And, as Elise said last night, if the fortune teller is perceived as a danger to residents, then approval from town council for the pier's demolition will be swift."

And he couldn't forget the chief. Maynard had certainly run into plenty of opposition over his request for more manpower in the department. The council members had all said they were basing their opinions on a lack of crime in Ocean Point.

"A sudden increase in crime, particularly violent crime, proves *them* wrong and *the chief* right," Mitch said quietly.

And then there was the fact that his boss despised psychics. The embarrassment the chief had endured in Sumter was big enough to make him leave a department he had built his career. And obviously there was still a ton of resentment based on his words today.

Mitch quickly folded the paper into a small square and placed it in his wallet for safekeeping.

He couldn't ignore the chief's order though. The fortune teller angle would have to be examined first. He pulled the telephone directory out from under his phone and flipped to the pages marked "N".

Mitch ran his finger down the page and stopped when he reached the listing for Ben and Kelly Naismith. He picked up the telephone and pressed the first few digits of the number, then stopped. Even though he hadn't known Ben well, he owed the man's widow a personal visit.

11:00 a.m.

Mitch shut the car door and turned to look at the house. The small yet attractive cottage had a welcoming feel. A hand painted sign beside the front door caught his eye. Although he was too far to make out the details of the sign, he could tell that there was a picture of a lighthouse beneath the words, "Ben and Kelly's Place."

His feet felt like lead as he walked up the narrow sidewalk. A maroon sedan with out-of-state license plates was parked in the driveway. Family members, no doubt.

He knocked on the door and waited. A few moments later the door was opened by a balding man in his mid to late sixties with puffy, red-rimmed eyes.

The man looked at him curiously. "Can I help you?"

Mitch pulled his badge from his shirt pocket and held it up for the man to see. "Good afternoon. I'm Detective Mitch Burns with the Ocean Point Police Department. I was hoping to have a few moments with Kelly if she is up to talking with me."

"Please come in. I'll go get Kelly."

Mitch stood in the front hallway and waited. Pictures of Kelly and Ben graced the walls, a young couple ready to face life together. He ran his hand over his eyes and through his hair. Nothing about these murders was easy. He couldn't bring people's loved ones back and at the rate he was going, he couldn't offer them justice either.

He looked up as he heard the sound of soft footsteps. Kelly Naismith walked toward him, her eyes hooded, her mouth contorted with grief. He held out his hand and grasped the woman's trembling fingers.

"I'm so sorry about Ben." He slid his hand around the woman's shoulder and pulled her in for a gentle hug. The tension in her body dissolved as she began to sob. Mitch held her for several moments until the crying stopped.

"I didn't know Ben well. He just started with our men's group at St. Theresa's a month or so ago and I have only made it a time or two since then. But it wasn't hard to miss the fact that he was a special guy."

He pulled a tissue from his shirt pocket and handed it to Kelly. The lump in his throat grew as he watched the woman wipe at the never ending stream of tears pouring down her cheeks.

"Have you found out who did this to my husband and why?" Her voice was raspy, hard to decipher.

"I'm working on that, and I promise you that I won't rest until I have that answer for you." He reached out and gently raised the woman's chin so as to look her straight in the eye. He needed her to know, to believe in him. "I know what you are going through right now. When my dad was murdered we had no answers and that destroyed my mother. I won't let that happen to you and I won't let that happen to Ben."

She shook her head slowly, a glimmer of clarity briefly resurfaced in her gaze.

"Kelly, I know that several of our officers spoke with you last night after Ben was found, but I have some questions for you, too."

"Okay."

"Where was Ben last night?"

"He got home from work around six and we had dinner together. Then I had a meeting to go to and Ben decided to go up on the boardwalk to see Mariah."

"The fortune teller?"

"Yes. Ben started going to her for readings a while ago and he seemed to get a lot of strength from it. It was one of the reasons that he joined the men's group at church. She said it would be good for him. You see, he was the kind of person that liked to have a road map in life and he believed that Mariah helped give him that."

"Did you see him after his reading last night, before he was killed?"

"No. I was expecting him home at any moment...and then the doorbell rang and the police were standing there and they told me that Ben was dead." The woman's voice broke, the tears returning. "I don't understand who would want to hurt him; he was the sweetest man I have ever known. He lived a good life, a clean life, a religious life...and this is what he got in return?"

The woman's voice increased in pitch as she continued to ask questions that had no answers.

"Ben couldn't walk past a child without saying something to make them smile. He volunteered in a homeless shelter once a month because he had a heart of gold. So why? Why did this happen to him?"

"I don't have that answer yet. But I will...you can count on it," Mitch said, although he knew his words were little comfort. "Thank you for your time and if you need anything at all, please call me."

He squeezed her hand once again and stepped outside. His heart was heavy with sadness. He wanted to spare Kelly the added heartache of not knowing so she could mourn her husband the right way. Not with anger and questions shadowing her grief. It was no way to live.

12:15 p.m.

His head was throbbing when he returned to the office. As hard as it was to watch the girls' families, seeing Kelly was even harder. It hit too close to home.

He replayed his conversation with Kelly over and over in his head. The Madame Mariah connection to all three victims was a nagging coincidence that wouldn't let go of his thoughts. But how it played into the murder was still anyone's guess. He reached for the still open phone book on his desk and flipped to the yellow page section. Madame Mariah's number was listed under the "Psychic" heading. He quickly dialed the number.

"Madame Mariah."

"Madame Mariah, this is Detective Mitch Burns with the Ocean Point Police Department. I have a few questions for you regarding a murder that took place last night."

"Tell me it wasn't Ben, please tell me it wasn't Ben," the woman said quietly.

"The victim's name was Ben Naismith." He decided to keep his hand hidden, act as if he didn't already know there was a connection between the two. It would make it easier to gage her reaction. "Did you know him well?"

"Yes. Ben is a regular customer of mine. He likes to have a peek at his future from time to time."

"When did you last see him?" the detective asked.

"Last night. He requested that I do a palm reading for him and I did," she said, her voice trailing off.

"And what did you 'see' when you read his palm?"

"I saw tragedy. I told him to be careful."

"Did you believe he was in danger?"

"Yes, I did."

"Why was he in danger?"

"I can only tell you that he, like the others, was punished for his visit to me."

"Punished? And what do you mean by 'like the others'?" Goose bumps were forming on his arms as he held the phone tightly.

"Both of the girls who have been killed, consulted me for a reading as well. But you know that, don't you?"

"Yes, I do."

"Well, they were punished for their visit, too."

Not knowing what to make of the woman's bizarre words, Mitch grabbed his notebook and jotted down her statement.

*They were punished for their visit.*

"That's all for now, Madame Mariah, but I must tell you that my questions for you are not over and I will be in touch again soon."

# 16

## 12:00 p.m.
## Tuesday, June 22

Elise deliberately chose a table near the back of the diner that would enable her to observe Daniel Johnson when he arrived. Sam had painted an interesting image of the developer in her mind and she was curious to see how it would match with the one she had in her own head.

"What can I get you, hon?"

She looked up to see an attractive waitress with teased blonde hair, a pink tank top and a tight denim skirt. The woman smiled at Elise, purple gum visible from time to time through the gap between her top front teeth.

"I'll take a glass of water for now, but I'd like to wait to order my lunch until my guest arrives," Elise said.

"Comin' right up." The woman leaned across the table and lowered her voice. "You've got the best seat in the house for people watchin' if you're into that kind of thing."

Was she ever. She nodded and smiled at the waitress.

The first person to walk through the door was a woman in her forties with a briefcase in one hand and a book in the other. She was dressed impeccably in a designer suit. Elise didn't need to think long. Lawyer. Single. Doesn't let anyone push her around.

She sat up straighter in the booth and eagerly waited for the next patron. Her observation skills had always been pretty good, and she enjoyed honing that ability whenever time permitted. At the very least it was an opportunity to be creative.

An elderly man was the next to come in to the diner. He was in his sixties and seemed to know the name of everyone in the restaurant. He was easy. Retired. Bored at home, so he found a second family at the corner diner.

"Here you go." The waitress placed a tall glass of water on the table in front of Elise. "It's fun, ain't it?"

"What's fun?" she asked distractedly.

"Trying to figure people out. I can kill me a whole day just tryin' to guess what makes 'em tick," the woman said as she snapped her gum. "The people that come through here—especially during the summer months—can be a real hoot sometimes."

"I try to figure out what they do for a living."

"Me too. I think everybody likes to guess. They just don't like to admit it. Well, I gotta go take an order. My name is Fran if you need anything before your friend shows up."

Elise reached for her water glass when the waitress left. The cold liquid felt good on the hot summer day.

The door opened again. This time it was a guy who looked like he'd be more comfortable at a Black Jack table with a cigar hanging out of his mouth and a thick gold chain around his neck. She'd always heard New Jersey was a haven for mobsters.

He picked some lint off his pinstripe suit and unbuttoned one more button on his shirt. She was right about the gold chain.

In one hand the man held a large tube, the other held a briefcase. He pulled Fran aside and whispered something in her ear. Elise was shocked to see the waitress point at her.

Daniel Johnson? Sam's description didn't appear to be too far off base.

As he approached her table, Elise stood up and extended her hand.

"You must be Daniel Johnson. It is a pleasure to meet you." She was not surprised by the strength of his handshake. She wondered if it had broken a few knuckles along the way. "I'm Elise Jenkins."

"Hello, Elise." He placed his briefcase and tube on the table and sat down. "I've been reading the articles that you've been writing since you came and I must say you're a very good reporter."

"Thank you, that's nice to hear."

"How do you like Ocean Point so far?"

"I love all of it...the beaches, the boardwalk, the people, the pace, the lifestyle, everything," Elise answered honestly. She was a little caught off guard by the man's seemingly genuine personality. Maybe Sam was wrong.

"I know what you mean. This is my second summer here since moving my business into the area and I love all the same things. That's why I want to help make Ocean Point even better."

"And you think that your condominium complex can do that?"

"Yes I do. I'm hoping that you can write an article that will help residents to see why my idea really is beneficial to everyone." He removed the cap from the cylinder tube and pulled out a large set of blueprints.

Before he could unroll the papers, Fran reappeared beside the table.

"What can I get you?"

She saw Daniel Johnson's eyes slide slowly up Fran's body, stopping briefly on her nametag.

"I'll take a double burger with bacon and cheese and a large side of fries. And I would love a cold draft beer when you get a second, Fran."

"I think I can find a second for you..."

Elise bit back the urge to laugh as she watched the waitress bat her long, false eyelashes at the developer. It never ceased to amaze Elise what was seen as a turn on by some women.

Fran wrote the order on her pad and then looked at Elise expectantly.

"I'd like a small garden salad with Italian dressing."

"You got it."

When the waitress left, Elise turned her attention back to Daniel Johnson.

"Are those blueprints of your condominium complex?"

"Yes, they are." He rolled them out on the table and turned them so Elise could see them clearly. "As you know, Ocean Point receives the vast majority of its revenue during the three months that make up the summer tourist season. Virtually every piece of property in this town is taken up by cottages, apartments, condominiums, year-round homes and businesses." His strong hands swept across the blueprints. "This lack of space leaves no room for additional growth or revenue. My condominium complex would make room for an additional 70 families to vacation here each week during those three peak months."

"Why the property where the first pier stands?" Elise asked. She was surprised by how professional he sounded despite his outward appearance.

"Good question, Elise. First of all, that portion of the pier invites losers, if I may be so blunt. The only vendors on that pier are repeat game operators and psychics. The people who tend to lurk there are the kind of people who can be detrimental to the image I believe this town tries to portray." Daniel Johnson leaned forward in his seat and looked straight into Elise's eyes. "And you must admit a condominium on that property would be fabulous with its Oceanside rooms and beach access. It's prime property."

"My predecessor interviewed a number of vacationers last year who disagreed with the plan to get rid of the first pier. And they weren't 'losers' as you say, but rather your average family vacationers."

The man's entire demeanor instantly changed from pleasant and mild mannered, to tense and abrupt. The Daniel Johnson that Sam had described was now front and center.

"The reporter the paper had before you was an idiot. Who cares what vacationers think; it's not their town."

"Actually I think the town *should* care very much what vacationers think since, as you said, the vast majority of the town's revenue is made from the tourist trade. Without them your condominium complex would be a moot point, don't you agree?"

"Listen here, Elise. If the first pier did not exist, there would be no room for the fortune tellers on the second pier because it is filled to capacity with vendors already," he said as his voice became more forceful and agitated. "Without the fortune tellers, those three innocent people who have been killed over the past few weeks might still be here, don't *you* agree?"

He grabbed the beer mug Fran had quietly set down in front of him and took a long, slow gulp.

"If that pier is demolished and I build my luxury condominium complex, the residents of this town will be able to walk the streets and beaches of their community without being in danger..."

It was Elise's turn to stare into his eyes as she searched the man's face for any indication that he was issuing a threat. The eyes she looked into were dark and clouded.

"I guess it's really up to the town council to decide. The first reading of your proposal is set to take place on Thursday evening. The final read will come sometime next month." She could hear the nervousness in her voice.

"Ohhh, I'm quite sure that they'll approve my plan. Why wouldn't they? People are dying because of those damn fortune tellers and if the council wants its residents and vacationers to be safe they'd be idiots not to do whatever it takes to make that happen."

# 17

## 8:30 a.m.
## Wednesday, June 23

She passed four or five cars before it hit her as being odd. The summer crowd arrived and departed on Saturdays, not Wednesdays. Yet it seemed as if every car Elise walked past was being packed to the gills with suitcases, beach chairs and boogie boards.

Curious, she reached into her handbag for a notebook and pen. A man was trying to cram a beach umbrella into his car just a few steps from where she stood.

"Excuse me. My name is Elise Jenkins with the Ocean Point Weekly and I was wondering if I could ask you a few quick questions."

"Sure, if you don't mind me packing my car at the same time."

"It looks as if you are heading out..."

"You bet I am. I'm worried about my family's safety." He struggled with the umbrella for a few more seconds and then finally took it back out. "If there's some kind of lunatic picking people off, I don't think we need to be here any longer."

She shouldn't have been surprised, but she was. The police needed to find the killer soon or Ocean Point would be ruined.

"When did your vacation start?" she asked him.

"The beginning of June. Every year we rent a house here for the entire summer. I commute to my job in the city during the workweek while my wife and kids enjoy the beach." He straightened up and took a momentary break from packing. "We love it here."

She jotted down his words and considered her next question.

"What is it about Ocean Point that's kept you coming back year after year?"

"The whole package deal. We love the lazy days on the beach and then hitting the boardwalk at night. And as you can probably tell, my kids love the games."

Her eyes followed the man's gesture toward his car. A mountain of stuffed toys in varying shapes and color took up precious space in the luggage area.

"But I want my family to be safe when I'm at work and I can't be sure of that anymore." He closed the trunk and turned to her.

"May I have your name and hometown for my article," she asked sadly.

"Nate Winters and I'm from Westchester County in New York."

"Thanks for your time."

She closed her notebook and continued on, realizing as she walked that she didn't have enough pages left to interview the number of people who were leaving.

# 18

## 9:00 a.m.
## Thursday, June 24

$\int$he didn't know why she was so excited for her morning with the mayor but she was. Subject shadowing was a journalism technique she learned in school, a way to bring a subject to life for readers. And she was eager to give it a try on a man who was new at an important position.

Elise pulled her purse strap higher on her shoulder and tugged at the fitted summer jacket she wore over a soft pink blouse. She didn't know what was on the mayor's agenda for the day so she made sure to dress as professionally as possible.

The brunette seated behind a glass-topped counter smiled at Elise from across the foyer area of the town hall. "May I help you?"

"Yes. My name is Elise Jenkins and I have an appointment with Mayor Brown today."

"The mayor is expecting you." The woman stood and pointed to the door at the end of a short hallway. "Go right in."

"Thanks." Elise pushed a wayward curl off her forehead and headed toward the closed door. When she reached the door with the mayor's nameplate, she knocked softly. A moment later the door swung open and she was face to face with the town's top dog.

"How are you this morning, Elise?"

"I'm doing great. Thank you again for allowing me to follow you around this morning. I'll do my best to stay out of your way."

"I'm honored that you would *want* to follow me around. I only hope I don't bore you too much."

She liked him. His eyes sparkled when he smiled and he seemed to genuinely enjoy her presence. It was nice to know that most subjects weren't going to be like Daniel Johnson.

"So, what do you want to do first?" he asked as he gestured toward the coffee pot in the corner of his office. "Do you want a cup?"

"No thank you. As for this morning, I would really like to just observe you as you go about your day."

"Oh. A day-in-the-life kind of thing."

"Pretty much. It seemed like a neat way to mark your first full month in office."

He nodded and reached for a small pink slip of paper on top of his desk.

"I guess I'll return a phone call I received from one of our council members earlier." He took off his suit jacket and settled into his desk chair. "It seems that everyone around here is terrified Ocean Point is going to fall apart because of the murders."

She thought of the cars she had seen heading out of town yesterday morning, the look of worry on the faces of the occupants.

"Do you think it will?" she asked.

"No. I have faith that everything will come around. The fortune tellers will leave and things will be back to normal."

"Do you really believe that the fortune tellers are at the root of this?"

"Each victim had consulted a psychic the night they were killed, right? Obviously there is a link there. So, get rid of them and maybe this will all stop."

"Do you think Johnson and Associates' proposal for a condominium complex is the answer?"

"It is certainly *one* answer. But an even better answer is for people to stop consulting psychics in the first place." He adjusted the knot in his tie and sat back. "There is no way they can know the future. It's just not possible."

Elise considered the mayor's comments while he returned the council member's telephone call. It wasn't hard to tell from the one sided conversation she was hearing, that the official was quite alarmed by the amount of vacationers leaving Ocean Point. She was intrigued by the way the mayor worked to placate the gentleman, repeatedly assuring him things would be okay. He sounded so confident it was hard not to believe him.

When the call was complete, Steve Brown stretched his arms over his head and sighed.

"You wouldn't believe how many of those calls I've been getting over the past week or so."

"I'm sure," she said knowingly.

The receptionist entered the room and handed the mayor a memo. While he looked it over, Elise took a moment to look around the office.

Steve Brown certainly had a nice touch. The large mahogany desk and high back leather chair conveyed a feeling of respectability while the countless personal photographs added a touch of warmth. An American flag in the corner of the room was displayed proudly and an old--and somewhat battered—homemade cross, served as a reminder of where Steve Brown got his strength and faith.

When the mayor had finished reading, Elise took the opportunity to inquire about some of the pictures she saw.

"Did you take all these?" she asked. She picked up a maroon and gold frame with a picture of two young boys wrestling on the ground.

"Yes, I did. Those are my sons. They're teenagers now, but they still wrestle around with each other on a daily basis. Unfortunately it's not in such a loving way these days."

"You're a good photographer," she said with admiration. The sunrise shot hanging to the left of his desk was one she would have loved for her apartment.

"Elise, I would like to run over to St. Theresa's for a moment to light a candle for the families of the victims." He reached for his suit coat and stood. "I would be happy to have you accompany me."

As they walked the two short blocks to church, Elise marveled at the way her subject seemed to run his life.

"You're very active at St. Theresa's, aren't you?" she asked as they approached the steps to the church. "I saw you giving out communion on Sunday."

"Yes. My religion is very important to me. I hope to become a deacon one day."

"Wow! That would be quite an undertaking. I always liked the deacons at the church in my home town. They seemed more reachable somehow and I think it was because they could be married and have families."

"It's nice to see a young person who seems to be so in touch with her thoughts," he said. They walked into the tiny room off the sanctuary where the prayer candles stood. "I've seen you at Mass every Sunday since you arrived."

"I was brought up Catholic and attended parochial school from kindergarten on up. It's in my blood, I guess."

She stood quietly off to the side as the mayor placed a dollar bill in the offering box beside the candles. He struck a match and lit a candle near the front of the arrangement. He knelt down at the small pew and quietly said a prayer. When he was done, he made the sign of the cross and stood.

"I feel so badly for the parents of the two girls and for Ben Naismith's wife. What a disappointment for them."

They were halfway down the block before the oddity of his last statement hit her. Somehow *heartbreaking* seemed like a more appropriate description.

# 19

## 7:15 p.m.
## Thursday, June 24

She circled the block for the sixth and final time, hoping to find a parking spot somewhere.  The town council meeting was set to start in fifteen minutes and she was going to be late if she didn't find one soon.

But there was still nothing.  With a sigh of disgust, Elise gave up and drove back to her apartment.  She had only a few minutes now to walk the five blocks back to the town hall building.  She half jogged and half walked until she rounded the last corner.

She was stunned to see the amount of people streaming through the front door of the meeting hall.  It was as if a rock band was throwing a free concert.

"Hi, Elise."

She looked to her right and saw Mitch Burns getting out of a squad car with Chief Maynard.  They had gotten a parking spot right in front of the building.

"Who do you have to know around here to get a spot like that?" she teased. The sparkle in Mitch's eye when he looked at her was impossible to miss.  She looked down quickly at the sidewalk, afraid he would see her excitement and run.  She had waited her whole life for someone to look at her like that and now that it was finally there, she was afraid.

"Why?  Where did you park?"

"My apartment."

"I had a feeling this was going to be a circus." He opened the door for her and gently guided her through it.

"Because of the murders?"

"Exactly.  People have been calling the station all week. They are freaked out about the fact that some serial nutcase seems to be running around town.  Can't say I blame them."

"I know what you mean. I've talked to countless tourists this week who are packing up and leaving because they are afraid." She looked into Mitch's gentle brown eyes and knew his worried look was a mirror of her own.

"I don't usually come to these meetings because that's the chief's job. But I figured there would be a lot of questions tonight and people are gonna want some answers. I'm just not sure we can give them the ones they want to hear."

When they entered the meeting room, it was obvious that this was no normal meeting. The relatively few chairs that had been set up for the public were only enough to accommodate some ten percent of the people who were there. Fortunately, the press table provided Elise with a place to observe and record everything that would transpire.

"It looks as if the meeting is about to start, so I better go sit up front by the chief. When this spectacle is over I would like to drive you home just to make sure you get there safely."

She saw the quick look of concern flash across his face before he walked away. He cared about her. And she cared about him, too. Unfortunately there was so much on both of their plates right now that she doubted it would turn into very much.

She sighed. Why couldn't the right guy and the right time ever happen at the *same* time? She wasn't sure she would ever find the answer to that question, but now was not the time to try. She placed her shoulder bag down on the press table and opened the packet with her name on it.

The agenda for the monthly meeting was relatively short, no doubt a result of recent events. The night was set to kick off with twenty minutes of public comments and questions, followed by a presentation by Johnson and Associates.

Her gaze moved quickly down the list of items for the night. A revised ordinance concerning sign specifications and a briefing from the police chief completed the evening's agenda.

"The June 24th meeting of the Ocean Point Town Council is now in order." Mayor Brown struck the long table with a gavel. "We will open the meeting up to residents for any comments and/or questions. However, we remind everyone that each person may have only three minutes to speak."

Elise looked around the crowded room. Most of the faces she saw looked sad and troubled. She noticed an elderly man in his sixties stand up and approach the small podium that faced the mayor and council.

"My name is Jack Smith and I've lived in Ocean Point since I was a young boy. I've raised my children in this town and my grandbabies visit us now. I've always seen this town as a safe place—but no more. In just two and a half weeks we've had three members of this community killed. I'm fearful for my life. I want to know what the police department is doing to stop this."

Chief Maynard rose to his feet and stood in front of the room.

"Mr. Smith, I empathize with your feelings. Although I haven't lived here as long as you have, Ocean Point is my home now, too. I'm just as concerned with what's happening here as you are. We don't have many answers right now, but we're working day and night to catch this person."

"Is it true, as has been reported in the paper, that each victim had consulted a fortune teller just hours before they were killed?"

"Yes, it is. We are exploring that aspect completely. If need be, we will do what we need to do to make psychics illegal in Ocean Point."

She shot a look in Mitch's direction. He sat ramrod straight in his chair, his right leg bounced furiously. It was pretty obvious from where she sat that he was as surprised as she was by what his boss was saying.

"Do you think these fortune tellers are to blame for all of this?"

"It's certainly suspicious, don't you think?"

"But why now? They've been a part of our boardwalk for over a decade and they've never caused a moment's problem to the best of my knowledge," the elderly man said. He was clearly bewildered by what he was hearing.

"They are trouble in a variety of ways. Look at the clientele they draw in...it's mostly troublemakers. Then consider the fact that we are dealing with three murders right now, all with a definite tie to a particular psychic."

Elise was stunned by the animosity apparent in the police chief's voice. He wasn't even trying to be impartial.

"There are some good and decent people who consult those same fortune tellers," yelled a man from the back of the room. "Not all the clientele are troublemakers. All you need to do is look at the victims to know that."

She was curious to hear what the chief's reaction to that statement would be. But it wasn't the chief who responded.

"We're not here to debate character issues right now," Mayor Brown said as he leaned forward in his chair. "Let's get on with the meeting. Mr. Johnson, if you would like to begin your presentation now..."

She shrank back in her chair as the man she had met for lunch two days earlier walked past on his way to the front. There were no two ways about it...he scared her.

Daniel Johnson placed a large sketch onto the easel beside the podium. The artist's rendering of the luxury condominium complex was beautiful.

"Thank you for giving me this opportunity to address you this evening." She watched as he unbuttoned the top button of his silk shirt. "I first addressed you last year concerning my proposed condominium complex. But when I saw the reception I received, I decided to pull back for a while."

He paused for a moment, looking at each council member before continuing. "I suspect things will be different now, in light of recent happenings involving the pier I am suggesting for demolition."

She wondered why he was making it sound as if he was just now bringing it up again when in reality he had brought it back up again *prior* to the first murder. He was a piece of work.

"The condominium complex I am proposing is a luxury building with all the trappings of a first rate community." He reached into his back pocket and pulled out a handkerchief. He wiped at the beads of sweat on his forehead. "My complex would contain seventy two and three bedroom units. Those units would allow seventy more families to vacation in our town each week during the summer season. Which, as you know, would bring more revenue to our town. More revenue means more money for our roads, schools, parks, and so on.

"The land I am proposing for my complex is the land now inhabited by the first pier of the boardwalk. That portion of the boardwalk is made up of me-too games and psychics, neither of which are huge moneymakers. In fact, I believe that demolition of this pier will be a good and *safe* thing for everyone in this town."

It bugged her the way he was playing on everyone's vulnerabilities. Especially when she considered the possibility that he may be *responsible* for putting the fear there in the first place.

When he finished, she watched as he stood in front of the council members and waited for them to do the first reading of his proposal. She couldn't help but wonder if the council members felt as intimidated by him and his stance as she did.

"The second and final reading on this proposal will be at our meeting next month." The mayor struck his gavel once more and then looked at Daniel Johnson. "Thank you, Mr. Johnson. If you would send an extra copy of that artist rendering to my office, I would like to hang it up where our constituents can see it."

Daniel Johnson nodded his head, a look of undeniable smugness evident on his face. He was clearly satisfied with the fact that he had not received any resistance to his plan. He thanked each council member by name and then proceeded to gather up his drawing. When he passed her table he stopped. His icy brown eyes bore into her face, his mouth contorted with controlled rage.

"That went well, didn't it?" he asked through gritted teeth.

She was suddenly very grateful for Mitch's offer to drive her home. She turned her eyes away from the man and focused on the meeting. After a few uneasy moments, he finally walked away.

"As you all know, it is time to vote on the chief's request for an increase in manpower for our police department," Mayor Brown said, looking around at each member of the council. "I will give Chief Maynard a moment to address you before I call for the final vote."

Again, Chief Maynard rose to his feet.

"Thank you, council members, for the careful consideration I know you have given this request over the past month. Before the murders happened, I believed we were understaffed in the department. These murders have only solidified what I already believe. I'm just sorry you had to have such an unfortunate illustration of our need."

The chief shifted his weight from one leg to the other and continued.

"I do believe that the funds needed to allow me to hire one or two extra officers per shift is money this town really can't afford *not* to spend."

Less than a minute later, Chief Maynard had the unanimous result he sought.

"This meeting is adjourned."

Elise saw the chief jump out of his chair and slap Mitch on the back in a celebratory gesture. But it was the look on the detective's face that surprised her. Mitch looked uncomfortable, almost wooden. Why wouldn't he be excited about having a little extra help around the station?

She would have to ask him that question when he drove her home later. But for now she needed to try and get a few words with the various council members. Tomorrow was deadline day again and she had a lot of space to fill.

When she had gotten all the quotes she needed, Elise returned to the press table to gather the rest of her belongings.

"Ready to go, Elise?"

"Sure. Where's the chief? Didn't you two ride over together?"

"We rode over together, but he's going out to celebrate with Daniel Johnson and a few other people."

They walked out to the squad car in silence.

She could feel the tension in the air; see the rigid way Mitch moved. "Are you okay?" she asked quietly.

"Just got a lot on my mind right now. I'm following so many different possibilities with these murders and I feel like my head is going to explode." He unlocked the door of the police car and held it open for Elise.

She sat down in the car and looked around. The closest she had ever gotten to a police car was during school field trips in elementary school. Except back then the driver wasn't nearly as cute.

Elise smiled at Mitch as he got into the car, hoped her presence would somehow lighten his stress for at least a few moments. "I noticed your expression during Daniel Johnson's presentation. He makes you wonder, doesn't he?"

"He sure does."

"I met him for lunch on Tuesday. He's very insistent that his project will save the residents of Ocean Point." She looked out the window as the car pulled into the road. The groups of people who had been inside the town hall building for the meeting now stood in smaller units outside. She couldn't hear their words, but it wasn't hard to imagine what they said. The murders in Ocean Point were the only topics of conversation these days. "Daniel Johnson is a very intimidating man."

"Did he say something to scare you?" Mitch asked quickly.

"If he wasn't threatening me, then there was a threatening tone," Elise replied as they pulled up in front of her apartment.

"Back off him for a while, Elise. Just in case he does have something to do with this."

She was surprised and flattered by the protective tone in the detective's voice.

"Do you think he *does* have something to do with this?"

"He's one of my possibilities right now. But, Elise, that's got to stay between you and me. Promise?"

"You can trust me. I promise," she said quietly. She so wanted to touch him and erase the worried lines that creased his handsome face. "It seemed like you weren't too crazy about the chief getting his request approved. But won't that help lighten your load right now?"

"The approval might make my life a whole lot easier in more ways than one, I'm afraid."

She searched his face for some indication of what he meant by that statement, but he did not offer any explanation for his words.

"I've got to get back to the station and get some more work done tonight," he continued. He rubbed a hand over his eyes and yawned. "I want to go to Ben Naismith's funeral tomorrow if I can find an hour to spare."

She squeezed his hand quickly and stepped out of the car.

"Take care of yourself, Mitch Burns."

# 20

## 11:00 a.m.
## Friday, June 25

He *wasn't surprised* to see how many people were there to pay their last respects. Although their paths hadn't crossed often, Mitch was well aware of the fact that Ben Naismith had been the kind of guy who would give the shirt off his back and the food from his plate to help someone else.

Mitch placed the plaid blanket alongside the piles and piles of contributions people had brought in tribute. Even now Ben was helping others. The donations were going to be given to a homeless shelter on Ben's behalf, a selfless gesture in honor of a selfless man.

Mitch took a seat in one of the center pews and waited for the service to start. There were surely a hundred people gathered in St. Theresa's that morning. Many of the faces he saw were familiar, nearly all of them touched personally by Ben's special ways. He noticed Chief Maynard sitting four rows up with a few of the council members, and Mayor Brown off to the side speaking to Ben's widow.

As the opening notes of the processional began, he rose to his feet. The site of the pallbearers carrying Ben's casket brought a renewed sense of determination. He was going to catch the monster that did this. And he was going to see that he paid dearly.

During the service, several people stood at the lectern and spoke of Ben. Mitch had heard that Ben was a selfless guy, but the endless stories of ways he helped people surprised him.

"I remember the day that Benjamin came to see me." Father Leahy spoke slowly, considered each word carefully. "He hadn't been raised in a religious home, didn't know much about God. But he realized his life held little meaning and so he sought answers. He listened to what I said, read the Bible, asked questions, and learned everything he could about our faith."

The elderly priest stopped for a moment and looked at Kelly. "As he learned and practiced Christianity, he saw the rewards from God. Kelly was the biggest. But instead of resting on what he had discovered, he sought to share it with people less fortunate than he. He was a missionary in every sense of the word, only his mission field was right here in our own backyards."

Father Leahy stopped speaking and nodded at a man in the second pew. The director of the Groverton Homeless Shelter introduced himself and shared a few memories of his time with Ben. Mitch tried to listen, but it was the quiet man who stood beside the director that caught his attention. He was oddly dressed in mismatched clothing, a look of profound sadness on his face. Mitch watched the man closely, curious as to his connection to Ben. He seemed wary, uncomfortable in his position at the front of the church. But when it was his turn to speak, his words were heartfelt.

"My name is Louis and I've spent many a night at the homeless shelter in Groverton where Ben volunteered. He always treated me like a human being, an equal." The man's eyes narrowed, his stance drooped. "Ben was a true gentleman in a world with very few."

The shelter's director slipped an arm around the man's shoulders and led him to a pew near the front of the church.

Mitch quietly cleared his throat and looked at the ceiling. It didn't matter that twelve years had passed since Dad's funeral. It seemed like yesterday at times. He swiped quickly at a tear that formed in his left eye, reluctant to let anyone in the church see him. Too many people counted on him for crimes that were happening now. Not something that happened in the past.

When it was Kelly's turn to speak, he listened closely to every pained word that left her mouth. But it was when she spoke of the children she and Ben would never have that he felt the tears start again.

Mitch closed his eyes and forced himself to think of something other than the words Kelly spoke. Father Leahy had once told him that he couldn't change what was in the past. He needed to look forward, pray for guidance. It was a lesson that applied as much to his life now as it did when he first consulted the priest four years ago. There wasn't anything he could do to bring back Susie or Cindy or Ben. He needed to look forward, concentrate on solving the crimes so there wouldn't be any more victims and so loved ones like Kelly could have answers.

Mitch prayed silently, a mantra that always helped him escape troubled thoughts. And gratefully, it worked once again.

When he opened his eyes, Kelly had returned to her seat. Her anguish was more than he could handle at that moment. He wanted so desperately to offer her a measure of comfort that would come with the knowledge of who and why. But he couldn't. Not yet anyway.

He looked at the piano as the first few notes of "Amazing Grace" began and noticed Ray Carlson. How the man could sit there and play that song just two weeks after the death of his own daughter was beyond Mitch's comprehension.

As the second verse of the hymn began, Mitch noticed a quiet commotion off to the side of where he stood. Chief Maynard and Mayor Brown were escorting a woman to a side exit, and from where he sat it didn't appear as if it were friendly. He strained to see around the open hymnals beside him, to catch a better glimpse of the woman's face. But it was no use. The only thing he noticed was the long caftan she wore with a simple pattern, and black hair in a bun.

"I'm surprised she actually showed up, knowing the rumors going around about her."

Mitch looked at the gentleman standing beside him.

"Who is that?" he whispered.

"That's Madame Mariah. She's the fortune teller that Ben saw just before he died." The man lowered his voice so only Mitch could hear him. "I guess the police chief and the mayor think her presence is inappropriate."

"Did you know Ben well?" He knew it wasn't the time to carry on a conversation, but he couldn't help himself.

"Yes. Kelly is my niece."

Mitch nodded, reached a hand to the man's shoulder and squeezed gently. They both turned back to their hymnals and finished the song. But Mitch's attention was no longer on the words he was singing. He wanted to walk out the same door the chief had gone through with the fortune teller but he couldn't. He didn't want his hasty retreat to call attention away from the person everyone had come to mourn.

When the service was over, Mitch turned once again to the man beside him.

"I'm sorry about your loss. I'm Detective Mitch Burns and I'm working very hard to find out who did this. Please know that."

The man held out his hand to Mitch and shook it firmly.

"I know that. And Kelly knows that as well. I was told you were out at the house the other day and I know your visit meant a lot to her. I just hope she didn't notice Madame Mariah being escorted from the service."

"I hope so too. I got the impression when we spoke that Ben and Madame Mariah were friendly with each other and that he respected her."

"He did. And Kelly is convinced that the fortune teller had nothing to do with Ben's murder. Frankly I find it a bit far fetched as well." The man patted Mitch on the back and then excused himself quickly so he could join Kelly's family in the receiving line.

Mitch started for the side door where the chief had gone out with the fortune teller, then stopped. His boss's actions only served to reinforce the animosity Mitch knew the man had for psychics like Madame Mariah. But just how far would that animosity drive him?

"Detective Burns?"

Mitch turned and saw the balding man he had met briefly at Kelly's house just a few days earlier.

"Hi. I'm sorry, I didn't get your name the other day."

"Frank Mertz. I'm Kelly's father. I was hoping you had some sort of lead or information that might help my daughter out right now..."

Mitch shook his head, searched for words that would bring comfort to the man. But there were none. "I am sorting through every piece of evidence I come across and I know it is going to happen. We're going to get him, you have my word."

If only he could have faith in his own words. So many people were counting on him to stop the killing. He took a deep breath and walked towards the end of the pew. His gaze fell on a man hunched over in a chair in a far corner of the church. He stepped to the right just enough to get a better view of the person and realized it was Father Leahy. Worried, he headed over to the priest.

"Father, are you okay?"

"I'm afraid not. I'm so deeply troubled by what is happening to my parishioners." The priest looked upward as he spoke. "I have presided over three funerals in two weeks and I feel so powerless. Susie, Cindy and Ben were all so faithful and good. I just don't understand what the Lord's plan is right now."

The normally upbeat man continued sadly. "Then, today, I watched as two of my parishioners removed a mourner from my church. I am saddened by the way people seem to be rushing to judgment."

"You saw that?"

"Yes, I did," the priest answered quietly. "I asked the men why they made the woman leave and our mayor said she did not belong in God's house."

Mitch reached out for the priest's hand and held it gently. The man's sickly pallor alarmed him. Normally very energetic and youthful, Father Leahy suddenly looked every bit of his seventy years.

"I'm doing everything I can to figure out who is doing this. I have some solid leads right now, Father, but I have to examine every aspect to make sure the right person is brought to justice for these crimes." He looked at the elderly priest with concern, hoped his words were bringing some sort of reassurance and comfort to the man he had come to depend on so heavily since moving to Ocean Point.

"I will say a special prayer for you, Mitch, so God may give you the wisdom and strength to see these investigations through. I will also pray for our parishioners so they may find it in their hearts to keep their minds open until you have completed your work."

"Thank you, Father."

# 21

## 9:30 a.m.
## Monday, June 28

They were all waiting in the conference room, their solemn faces a mirrored reflection of her own.

"Sorry, I'm late everyone," Elise said, placing her notebook and pen on the table.

"You're not late." Sam gestured toward the wall clock over the doorway. "We're all early for once."

Sam's normally jovial mood was replaced by a quieter demeanor. He skipped his usual lighthearted small talk and got right down to business.

"We've had more news to cover in the past three weeks than I would have ever hoped to see. Each of you has been the consummate professional in these matters and I'm proud to have you on my team." He removed his glasses and rubbed his eyes. "I want to continue working *with* the police department to help solve these cases, not use our reporting as sensationalism. And we're doing a very good job in that regard so far."

He handed an agenda to each of them.

"Let's hold off on talking about the murders for the time being, and discuss some lighter stuff first." He looked around at his small staff, his gaze stopped on Elise. "Elise, nice job on your inside look at the new mayor."

"Thanks, Sam. He's a nice man."

"Self-righteous Steve?" Dean leaned his arms on the conference table and looked at Elise, his gaze a mixture of disbelief and curiosity. "I'll never understand how that guy got elected. He spouts Bible verses the way most people recite movie lines. He's always hurling biblical stuff around like he's some sort of guru."

"His religion is certainly important to him, but I wouldn't call him a guru." Her defensive tone seemed to surprise everyone, including herself. "He's a nice guy."

Dean shrugged his shoulders and leaned back in his chair. She looked down at her notations quickly, looking for some way to diffuse the sudden tension she felt in the room.

"My luncheon with Daniel Johnson was interesting, to say the least. I talked to some people after the council meeting Thursday night and several of them are considering the possibility of a picket against his proposal."

"Oh, that'll go over big," Sam said with sarcasm. "Old Danny Boy will blow a fuse if people screw with his request."

"I think so too," Elise said. "These residents I spoke to are furious that he wants to bring more vacationers into Ocean Point. They are grateful for the business each summer and don't want to see that jeopardized in any way, but they don't think we need any more people coming in."

"I think there are a lot of people who feel that way," Karen said. The society reporter crossed her legs and sat up straight in her chair. "Most people I speak with want things to stay the same. They are adamant about not wanting any more outsiders in this town."

"When are they planning this picket?" Sam asked.

"They're aiming for this Thursday if they can get the support they need."

"I think the expression on Daniel Johnson's face will be the real photo op there," Dean mused.

"He certainly sees the recent murders and their apparent tie-in with the fortune tellers as his ticket to building that condo," Elise said. "And he's playing it for everything it's worth."

"I bet he is," Sam said, his scowl a clue to the disgust he felt.

"Speaking of the fortune teller thing, did you guys hear about Madame Mariah's hasty exit from Ben Naismith's funeral on Friday?" Elise turned her gaze to look at the normally quiet sports writer. It was rare that he spoke of anything other than sports. But she had come to learn that when Tom *did* speak, it was usually worth listening to. "She got a personal escort out of the church, though I dare say it wasn't a requested escort."

"What do you mean escorted out?" Elise asked.

"My friend was there and he said that the lady showed up halfway through the service and sat down. When Chief Maynard and Mayor Brown saw her, they evidently went berserk. They went over to her and pretty much dragged her out of the church."

"I guess they didn't want to hear their fortunes, huh?" Dean asked in a wicked tone. He shoved a donut hole into his mouth and looked around with a grin.

"It certainly seems as if that woman is the prime suspect, at least in the eyes of many Ocean Point officials." Sam shook his head slowly as he spoke. "I just think the whole scenario smells too fishy."

"I agree totally," Elise said. "I think she's being set up as the fall guy."

"Don't you mean fall *psychic*?" Dean quipped.

11:00 a.m.

Mitch looked at the crime scene photographs and personal information in front of him for the hundredth time. But it didn't seem to matter. Nothing new jumped out at him that could help him solve these vicious crimes.

He thought back over the week and about the council meeting Thursday night. Daniel Johnson had seemed so smug when he was giving his condo pitch. It was like he knew he was going to win.

"Maybe Elise is right," he said under his breath. "Maybe this creep is so desperate for his damn condo that he'll do anything to get the council members to vote in favor of tearing down the first pier."

It wasn't too long ago that someone at Mia's had suggested to him that the small fire at Madame Mariah's last year may have been deliberately set in an attempt to destroy her business and the entire pier. Could that failed attempt have been the catalyst for something more drastic?

"Daniel Johnson would certainly have had motive for this crime as well," Mitch mumbled. He thought back to last year. It was after the fire--and the council's less than enthusiastic response to the proposal—when the developer first backed down. Until now. Here he was, a year later, trying to play on the town's fears in order to get his way. And, once again, Madame Mariah's business is the target.

And Elise was afraid of him. She seemed to suspect him and he certainly seemed like a likely suspect. Maybe it was time to pull Daniel Johnson in for questioning concerning the murders. Every time they had spoken to that point was in regards to the condominiums.

But then there was the chief. He hated psychics. He wanted more manpower in the department but there wasn't enough crime to justify the added officers. Now there was, and he was getting his bigger department.

Mitch was ashamed of the brief thought that flashed through his head. But he couldn't ignore it. If the killings suddenly stopped now that the chief's request was approved, he would have to do much more than just wonder about his boss.

"And what about Madame Mariah?" He rose to his feet and walked toward the photographs of each victim. "Every one of them consulted her for a reading and she warned each of them of tragedy. Then, whamo, they're dead."

He paused momentarily as a flood of thoughts raced through his mind. He found himself recalling the psychic's bizarre words when they had talked on the telephone. But what the hell could she mean by being punished for their visit?

He knew that if she wasn't involved in the murders then it meant she really could see the future. And he didn't believe in that stuff at all.

He looked at the clock on his desk and pushed the intercom button on the bottom of his phone.

"What do you need, Mitch?"

"Is the chief around?"

He grabbed his badge and locked his desk drawer.

"Nope. He's sitting down with the big wigs at town hall trying to work out the details of our soon-to-be recruiting efforts. Shouldn't be much longer, though."

"Okay. Will you please leave him a message for me?"

"Sure thing. Shoot."

"Tell him I'm heading home to get some rest. I'm going to be doing a little checking around tonight and I'll be in touch with him in the morning."

"Doing a little undercover work, huh?"

"You got it. Thanks."

Maybe he'd finally find some answers where Madame Mariah was concerned.

# 22

## 7:30 p.m.
## Monday, June 28

Although he was fairly certain Madame Mariah wouldn't notice him, he didn't want to take any unnecessary chances. His khaki shorts and polo were a safe bet for blending in, but his lack of tattoos didn't help. Maybe he could pass as a tourist.

He pulled his baseball cap a little lower on his forehead and quickened his stride. The boardwalk was busy. Everywhere he looked he saw a familiar face and hoped they didn't notice him. The staff intern, Mayor Brown, Elise's boss, Chief Maynard, Daniel Johnson, and even Father Leahy were out in force. But they hadn't seemed to notice him.

Once he was safely past the faces he knew, Mitch stopped to grab a bite to eat. It was going to be a long night and he needed something to keep him alert.

"Hey, how's it going?" He tried to keep his head down as he addressed the concession worker. The fewer people that recognized him, the more likely it was his cover wouldn't be blown. "I'll take a cheese steak with onions and two Yoo-Hoos."

"Comin' right up!"

Mitch looked out toward the beach as he waited. The white foam of the waves broke up the darkness, their rhythmic sound more noticeable at this end of the boardwalk. It was more peaceful down here, inviting. A great place for a long walk with Elise. He would give anything to get these murders solved so he could put in a real effort where she was concerned.

He felt a smile creep across his face and chuckled. Aunt Betty always said he would know when he found the right girl. And he couldn't help but feel he may have finally done that.

"Here you go. Enjoy."

Mitch nodded at the worker and grabbed the white bag. He headed immediately toward a vacant bench just a few feet from Madame Mariah's doorway. The vantage point was perfect for seeing everyone who came and went from the woman's booth. He sat down, stretched out his legs and reached inside the bag next to him.

10:00 p.m.

Scott Levine was almost done with his novel, but he knew he needed a better perspective on the fortune teller who entered briefly into the ending. So it was with a pad of paper in one hand and his lucky pen in the other that he set off for the boardwalk.

He eyed the countless parking lots closest to the boardwalk but refused to pay the six bucks to use any of them. The remote alleyway four blocks away would be just fine. With any luck he'd be trading in the 1975 Chevy wagon for a Porsche in a few months and then maybe he'd just park *on* the boardwalk next time.

Laughing at the image, he tossed the cola bottle he had just finished onto the pavement in front of him and headed toward the bright lights and carnival noises of the nearby amusement piers.

Madame Mariah was going to be perfect for his character research. He'd been hearing a lot about her lately and figured she would be as good a choice as any to teach him about the world of psychics.

As he approached the first pier, Scott began the mind clearing exercises he found necessary to transform himself into the award winning author he knew he would soon be. They worked just fine until he saw the guy sitting on the bench drinking Yoo-Hoo. It really bugged him to see guys like that lounging around without a care in the world. Must be nice to not have to worry about a paycheck.

He could feel his anger growing, his task at hand forgotten. But he couldn't let that happen. The world was full of lazy guys who had the world by the pants. He'd be lounging around like that too, once his novel sold. Only he would be drinking something a lot classier than Yoo-Hoo.

When he finally reached Madame Mariah's House of Fortunes, he was grateful to see only one other person in the waiting area. He looked around the room. A sign propped up on a table in the corner caught his eye. Ten bucks to have a fortune done? He could feel his anger rising to the surface. Why was it that everyone was out to screw him?

But it would be worth it to finish the book right. And besides, he thought, it would probably be a tax deduction later on. Research expenses.

Less than 15 minutes later it was his turn.

"Would you like a Tarot Card reading, a palm reading or shall we take a look at the Crystal Ball?" the mysterious looking woman asked him.

He could feel his creative juices flowing as he savored everything about the atmosphere. He chose a palm reading.

"Take a seat," the woman said. She pointed to a worn chair across from where she was now seated.

With the prices she charged, he couldn't help but wonder why she didn't have a better chair for her clients.

He sat down and faced her, suddenly aware of how nervous he felt.

"What line would you like me to read first?"

"What line?"

"You have three main lines in your palm," she explained slowly. "You have a Heart Line, a Head Line, and a Life Line."

"Let's go with my Heart Line first." He soaked up every detail of the woman's face as she bent over his palm, studied the crisscrossed lines that seemed etched into her skin.

"I see a very lonely life. No one very special, although there was someone not too long ago. You thought there was a future with this person but it did not come to pass."

He shifted in his seat. How could she know that? And then he remembered the wedding notice that had been changed in the paper after he was left standing at the altar.

"Instead, you fill your life by creating scenarios," she continued. "These creations are your passion now."

He thought of his book.

"Now, I will read your Life Line." The woman tilted the gooseneck lamp on the table so it would shine more brightly on his palm.

"Oh dear." All color in the woman's face drained as she spoke, her skin almost ashen in its appearance.

"What?" Scott asked. He found the woman to be very amusing in her performance. But those same theatrics probably explained the lines in her face.

"You are in danger, grave danger. You must be very careful when you leave here," she said, her voice rising with each subsequent word.

"What kind of danger?" he asked. He knew his words sounded sarcastic but he couldn't help it. This was ludicrous.

"I'm afraid for you and your safety. Please be very careful." She rose to her feet and waved in the direction of the curtain. "You should go now."

"No way. I gave you ten bucks to do this reading and I want you to read the Head Line too."

He saw the bewildered stare the woman gave him and he met her gaze head on.

"Take your ten bucks back," she shouted, shoving the crinkled bill he had just given her back into his hand.

Now that was what he called cheap research.

10:55 p.m.

Mitch looked at his wristwatch. His stakeout was a bust so far. In all the time he had sat on the bench, he had only seen a handful of people actually go in and out of Madame Mariah's. And based on snatches of conversation he was able to pick up as they walked by, he was able to deduce that most of them were tourists.

He couldn't ignore the discrepancy he saw. The majority of the fortune teller's clients seemed to be tourists, yet each and every murder victim was a resident of Ocean Point.

He heard whistling and looked up. A balding, heavy set guy in his mid thirties walked out of Madame Mariah's, whistling. A smug smile pulled at the man's lips. Whatever had happened with the fortune teller had apparently made his night. Mitch took a few gulps of his second Yoo-Hoo and watched curiously as the man walked by. The tune he whistled was familiar.

Mitch strained to pick out the music. After a few more notes, he figured it out. "We're in the Money."

He watched the man walk down the Second Street steps until he disappeared out of sight. Mitch shrugged and turned his gaze back on Madame Mariah's door.

11:05 p.m.

"What a night," Scott Levine said under his breath as he pulled his car key out of his pocket and inserted it into the car door.

He wiggled the key and swore loudly. Wrong one. He held the ring up and tried to identify the correct key in the darkened alley. A noise from behind made him spin around.

He saw the angry face, the arms raised in the air, the wooden object clutched in the tightened fist. Trying to duck out of the way, he tripped on the cola bottle beside his car.

He struggled to his feet and looked up just as the piece of dark wood headed straight for his head. The pain he felt next was excruciating and he moaned in agony as he took his final breath.


11:15 p.m.


Standing over Scott Levine's body, he could feel the overwhelming satisfaction that came with accomplishment. It had to be done. There was no other way.

He bent down and pulled the piece of wood from the man's forehead. He wiped off the wood with a wet cloth and looked around the deserted alley to make sure he had not been seen. Once he was certain he was safe, he bent down once again. With careful precision he extended the man's index finger before placing the motionless hand back down on the pavement.


11:50 p.m.


Mitch grabbed his food wrapper and headed for the trash can on the other side of the boardwalk. He felt like a fool for wasting so much time. He had learned nothing, absolutely nothing.

Except that bad publicity doesn't always hurt one's business.

The sound of his cell phone ringing caught him off guard. He completely forgot he even had it with him. Fumbling for the phone he had tucked away in the pocket of his shorts, he flipped it open.

"Detective Burns."

It was like a bad movie that wouldn't stop. The now familiar words on the other end of the line were like a punch in the gut.

"I'll be right there."

# 23

## 9:25 a.m.
## Tuesday, June 29

She placed the bag of donuts on Sam's desk and sat down. In her wildest dreams she could never have imagined the kind of upheaval she had witnessed at the police department that morning.

"Good morning, Elise. To what do I owe this honor?"

She looked up at her boss and shrugged.

"What's wrong?" he asked quickly.

"There's been another murder."

Sam's mouth dropped open, disbelief in his eyes.

"When? Where?"

"Last night. A few blocks from the boardwalk," she said. "They found him lying next to his car."

She watched as Sam sat down and rested his head in his hands. He looked so tired and sad. She opened the bag of donuts in front of her and offered him one.

"For me?" Sam asked.

"Yup. I figured you could use a surprise. I'm just sorry it had to come with such horrible news."

"So am I." He reached into the bag and pulled out a chocolate covered donut. "Who's the victim?"

"His name is Scott Levine and he's from Ocean Point." She reached into the bag on the floor by her chair and pulled out a tall cup of coffee for Sam and a cup of hot chocolate for herself.

"Scott Levine? I know him," Sam said in disbelief. "He's in my critique group."

"He was a writer, too?"

"Yeah, he was almost done with a mystery novel he's been working on for over a year. He was positive it was going to be the one that made him famous."

She studied her boss as he spoke, trying to get a read on how close the two had been.

"I'm sorry, Sam."

"It's okay. We were in the same group but we didn't really hang out together. Scott was kind of a tight wad." He wiped a drop of coffee off his lip and continued. "He was one of those guys who was just obsessed with money."

She was glad to hear they weren't close. Somehow, the thought that Sam had been directly affected was more than she could handle right now. She took a quick sip of hot chocolate and selected a glazed donut for herself.

"Hot chocolate?" Sam asked with a grin.

"Yup."

"It's almost July, Elise."

"Chocolate is never out of season."

They both sat in silence for a few moments, each deep in thought. Sam finally broke the quiet.

"So how'd you find out about Scott?"

"I stopped in at the police station this morning before I picked up the donuts," Elise said. "I wanted to check the police logs so that I wouldn't have to worry about them on deadline day."

"Good thinking."

"Anyway, the station was just crazy. Everyone seemed to be in a panic, not knowing what to do or where to start. I pulled one of the interns aside and that's when I found out about the victim. Apparently the Medical Examiner's preliminary report indicates that the same type of weapon was used on Scott as the other three murder victims."

Sam set his coffee cup down and leaned forward in his chair.

"I imagine the F.B.I. will be getting involved here soon. Four murders in as many weeks is usually the work of a serial killer. And it won't be long after that before the big national news magazines start working our turf."

She hadn't thought of that. The last thing she wanted was for a big name magazine to come in and show them up.

"Is there something that..."

A knock at Sam's door prevented the conversation from going any further. Debbie, the receptionist, stood in the doorway.

"Yes, Debbie?"

"There's a call for Elise on line three. The guy says he's the one who found the body last night."

Sam pushed his phone toward Elise and motioned for her to take the call there.

"I'll be right here if you need me," he said reassuringly.

She was glad Sam was there. Sitting in a classroom listening to a teacher talk about situations like this was not the same as actually being in the middle of it. She hoped his presence would keep her from screwing it up somehow.

She picked up the phone and pressed the line three button.

"This is Elise Jenkins. I understand you found the murder victim's body last night, is that right?" Elise asked, smiling gratefully at Sam as he pushed a notebook and pen in front of her.

She listened carefully to the voice on the other end of the telephone. The young man was obviously on a high, pumped up by the first hand information he had.

"You found him at 11:30...four blocks from the boardwalk...head wound..."

She wrote quickly, trying to keep up with everything she was hearing.

"His finger was what? Where were you when the police made that remark?"

She saw Sam's quizzical look and knew her last few comments had caught his attention.

"Thanks so much for calling me with this information. Can I have your name and number in case I think of any further questions?" She jotted down the man's information then looked up at Sam quickly. She mouthed a "wow" and rolled her eyes upward.

"What did you get?" Sam asked as she returned the phone to its cradle.

"This guy, Mark, said he found the body last night around 11:30 when he was walking his dog. He said the victim had a massive wound to his forehead. What's interesting is he noticed that the victim's right index finger was extended outward, as if he were pointing at something.

"When the police arrived on the scene, he overheard one of them commenting specifically about the finger. Apparently, the odd position of Scott Levine's finger was exactly the way they found each of the other three victims."

"'Wow' is right."

"I just wonder why Detective Burns never mentioned the finger similarity after the other murders," Elise said curiously.

"More than likely they are holding that piece of evidence back as a way to weed out the real killer."

"Well, now that I know about it, I'm going to ask Mitch about it and see what he says." She stood and headed for the door. "If he asks me to keep it quiet, though, I think we should honor that request."

"Absolutely. I want to see this nut case caught as much as the next guy and I've been around the block enough times in my career to know that what *we* do can impact a case significantly. I want it to be in a positive way."

She marveled at his calmness. Most editors would be screaming at everyone to get out there and get the story. But Sam was a human first, an editor second. And it was why she had clicked with him immediately. "Well, I'm gonna get back to work now."

"Hey, Elise, thanks for the coffee and donuts," Sam said. "I'm really glad you came here. You're doing a great job."

When she returned to her desk she picked up the telephone and dialed the Ocean Point Police Department. She asked for Detective Burns and then waited.

"Detective Burns." His voice sounded distracted. He was under so much stress right now and she could hear it in his voice.

"Hi, Mitch. It's Elise. How are you holding up?"

"I don't know. I just want to catch this creep before another person has to die."

"I just got a call from the guy who found the body last night. He told me the man's right index finger appeared to be pointing outward."

"Damn!"

"He said he overheard someone in the department commenting that it was just like the other victims."

"Damn it!"

"I take it you were wanting to keep that under wraps?"

"I was..."

"Don't worry, Mitch, I won't print it."

She could hear the audible sigh of relief from the other end of the telephone.

"You have no idea how glad I am to hear you say that, Elise. You're truly a class act, you know that?"

She could feel her face beginning to blush.

"What could he have been pointing to?"

"I don't know. I've looked at the crime scene photographs over and over again trying to figure out what each of the victims could've been pointing to and it's different in every case."

"Could the killer be posing their finger like that?" Elise asked. She moved her index finger around while they spoke.

"I've thought of that. Maybe it's a calling card," Mitch said. "Very often serial killers leave a kind of calling card behind."

She stared at her finger as she stretched it straight out over and over. Maybe they weren't pointing at all.

"I'm looking at my finger right now. Maybe they aren't pointing but rather using their finger to indicate the number one."

The complete silence that followed made her wonder if they had been disconnected. But just as she prepared to hang up she heard the sound of life on the other end.

"Man! This whole time I've been beating myself up over what each victim could have been pointing to, and never once did I consider that possibility."

"But what could number one mean?" she asked.

"I don't know, but I'll let you know when I come up with something."

"Good luck."

"Thanks for the call. It feels good to talk to someone about this and you may have really helped me out with this whole finger thing."

She hoped so. He obviously needed a break.

"You're going to solve this, Mitch. I just know it," she said softly. "Take care and I'm sure we'll be talking soon."

"I hope so."

10:35 a.m.

"One...one...one." He looked down at his own finger and repeated Elise's suggestion over and over to himself.

It was funny how each body shot looked so different to him now. Finally free of the pointing idea, he could consider everything in a completely new light. He grabbed his recorder and turned it on.

"Maybe the victims were trying to give some sort of clue as to who did this." He grabbed the full body shot of the first victim, Susie Carlson. "But she was face down. The Medical Examiner was certain she had not seen her attacker. And if he was right about that

120

as I'm sure he was, then the victim would have been unable to leave a clue."

He pulled the list of suspects out of his wallet and unfolded it. His eyes lingered over each name.

"I can cross Madame Mariah off the list because she never left her booth last night," he said, lining through the psychic's name. But just because she didn't do it herself, didn't mean she couldn't have hired someone else to do her dirty work. He rewrote the psychic's name.

The next person on his list was Daniel Johnson. He had seen him at the boardwalk last night. But so was the last person on his list—Chief Maynard.

"He's gotten his extra cops, so the motive would have to be wrong," he muttered quietly under his breath. "But there's still the humiliation he suffered at the hands of a psychic."

He crossed out the original motive and replaced it with a single word. Revenge.

Elise's voice raced through his mind, his words echoing hers. "One...one...one." He looked again at his finger as he spoke, envisioned what *he* would mean if he used a gesture like that.

"Oh my God. Could it mean *first?* As in *first pier?*"

It was as if he had been hit with a bucket of cold water. The file on Johnson and Associates he had requested sat on his desk, untouched. He flipped it open and began reading in earnest.

# 24

## 8:15 p.m.
## Wednesday, June 30

It *was hopeless.* There was absolutely nothing worth watching on television. Sighing, Elise pushed the off button on the remote and watched the picture vanish into blackness.

She was bored. And it was driving her crazy.

She rested her head on the back of the couch and looked around the small family room. A painting of some sort would look so good to the left of the door, she thought. But she needed to go slowly, save a little money first. Unfortunately, patience had never been her strong suit.

The large stuffed dog perched in the corner of the entryway brought an instant smile to her lips. The way Mitch had broken the plates one after the other was impressive. And in three quick throws, the stuffed dog had become her prized possession. It was a reminder of a happy time, and a hope for something special in the future with a very nice guy.

She grabbed the paperback sitting beside her on the couch and willed herself to read it. Just because they had gone on the boardwalk together for a few hours did not mean anything was going to come out of it in terms of a relationship. She flipped open the book and began to read.

Two pages into the first chapter the telephone rang.

"Hello?"

"Elise?"

"Yes?" she asked, straining to hear the hushed voice.

"Elise, this is Madame Mariah."

Shocked by the identity of her caller, Elise dropped her book and sat straight up on the couch. Why was Madame Mariah calling her?

"What can I do for you?"

"I don't know what to do. I'm very scared for my clients."

"Because of the three murder victims who had consulted you prior to their deaths?"

"*Four* murder victims."

Elise tightened her grip on the phone and swallowed over the lump that appeared instantly in her throat.

"Four? You mean you saw Scott Levine before he died, too?"

"I believe so, yes."

"Tell me what happened," she said. She wanted to know more, yet was fearful of what she would hear.

"I tried to warn him that he was in danger. But he thought it was a joke, talked only about the money he had spent on the reading."

Sam had mentioned that he was obsessed with money.

"Madame Mariah? Do you really see these things when you do a reading?" She knew her voice sounded childlike when she asked the question. But she had to know. It couldn't be a coincidence any longer.

"I have a gift of seeing the past, the present, and the future. In the vast majority of my readings I see good things...happy things. But these four people had such darkness about them that I feared for their safety. Sadly, I was right."

The genuine sadness and concern in the woman's voice was undeniable. She was obviously no more responsible for these murders than Elise was. Or else Elise was as naïve as her mother always said.

"The police are working on this case around the clock and I really believe they will find the person responsible for these crimes," Elise said, trying hard to inject as much reassurance into her voice as she possibly could.

"I just feel so awful because they were all punished for their *visit to me*," whispered the psychic.

There she goes again, Elise thought. Why did she have to be so cryptic, so strange?

"I don't know what you mean when you say that," she pleaded.

"That is all I can see. I must go now."

"Thank you for calling, Madame Mariah."

She stared at the wall for a few moments, the receiver still in her hand. Everything was just so messed up. She hated not having any answers. She hated the fact that so many innocent people were suffering. But there was nothing she could do.

She sighed and hung up the phone. Maybe her book would help distract her.

Four chapters later she realized she hadn't absorbed any of the words she had read. No matter how hard she tried to concentrate, her mind kept going back to the same thing over and over again.

The stuffed dog. And Mitch Burns.

"Maybe I should get a reading," she said softly. "Maybe Madame Mariah can tell me if she sees a man in my life sometime between now and when I hit 50."

# 25

## 10:30 a.m.
## Thursday, July 1

She pressed the save button on her keyboard and sat back in her seat. One more story finished.

"Hey, Elise," Debbie yelled from behind her desk across the room. "Just got a call from some chick. Town hall is being picketed."

She wasn't surprised. The residents she had spoken to after the town meeting were determined to do it. She reached for her notepad and pen and stood up. If she hurried, she could get some quotes and have the story written by mid day.

"Thanks, Debbie. I was told this might be coming."

She passed the receptionist's desk as she headed for the door. She liked Debbie a lot. She was always on top of things and managed to act as a great filter for the unimportant phone calls that came into the paper on a daily basis.

"Where are you off to?" Sam walked in the front door just as she turned her in/out card over.

"Those residents I told you about at our staff meeting got their picket together. I guess they're walking in circles outside town hall as we speak."

"You head on over and I'll see if I can track Dean down and send him over, too." Sam walked toward the darkroom and stopped. "A picket outside town hall will make a great front pager for Sunday's paper."

She stepped out into the brilliant sunshine and breathed in slowly. One of her favorite things about living near the ocean was the smell of the salty sea air. The sunny days, constant ocean breeze, and endless blue skies left little room for negativity. She forced herself to pick up the pace as she crossed Sandcastle Place and turned down

Sand Dune Lane. She loved the street names in Ocean Point, each one a reminder of the town's proximity to the Atlantic Ocean.

When the town hall finally came into view she could see the demonstrators walking in a wide circle in front of the building. Many of the picketers carried large posters with brightly colored words written in big block letters. She was impressed by the group's peaceful manner as they worked to get their sentiments across.

The first picketer she reached was a silver haired gentleman. He walked quietly, carrying a poster with the words, "Leave The First Pier Alone." Elise tapped him on the shoulder.

"I'm Elise Jenkins with the Ocean Point Weekly. Can I ask why you've decided to picket today?"

"Gladly. I've lived in Ocean Point for nearly 50 of my 58 years and I've watched this town grow larger each summer as everyone tries to think of new ways to accommodate more tourists. I'm not a fool, I know how important those summer dollars are to our community and our schools, but I think we're doing just fine the way we are right now. We don't need seventy more families in here each week and we most certainly don't need to tear down the first pier. That pier has been standing since my daddy helped build it some 45 years ago."

"You don't believe the first pier is the root of the recent rash of homicides in our town?" she asked.

"I most certainly do not. Madame Mariah has been working on that pier for a number of years and we've had no trouble from her at all," he said, scratching his forehead. "I don't believe she has anything to do with those deaths."

"Thank you, sir. May I have your name for my article?"

"Russ Shooler."

She heard the sound of a shutter firing behind her and turned around.

"Hey there, Dean." She pointed at the man she had just finished interviewing. "I got some good quotes from that gentleman in case you want to get a shot of him."

Dean nodded and started shooting.

"Excuse me," Elise said, tapping a young girl on the shoulder as she passed by with a sign. "I'm with the newspaper and was wondering if I could speak with you for a moment."

The girl put her sign down and walked over to a shaded bench a few feet away. She reached into a backpack and pulled out a water bottle.

"It's hot out here."

"It sure is," Elise agreed. "What made you want to come out here on a hot day like this to voice your opinion on the proposed condo project?"

"I don't care if they build another condo in town or not," she said between gulps of water. "What I'm upset about is where they want to *put* the condo."

"Because of the pier?"

"Yeah. If they put some luxury condo on the beach, you can bet they'll try to make that portion of the beach private. Right now you can step off the boardwalk and sit by the water whenever you want, and I don't want to see that change."

Elise wrote the girl's comments in her notebook. They made perfect sense.

"Thanks for your time. Can I get your name?"

"Mel Cronin."

She watched as the girl picked up her sign and joined the picket line once again. It was neat to see people of all ages fighting for what they believed in. Elise caught Dean's eye and pointed in the girl's direction. He turned the camera and snapped a few more pictures.

11:35 a.m.

"May I speak with Daniel Johnson?"

"May I tell him who's calling?"

"Elise Jenkins with the Ocean Point Weekly."

She drummed her hands on the desk as she waited. The quotes she had gotten from the picketers were good, but she knew Daniel Johnson's reaction to them would be even better. She looked up at the wall clock in the editorial room and sighed. Five minutes later he finally came on the line.

"Sorry to keep you waiting, Elise."

It was funny how sarcasm could be so easy to pick up even when you didn't have a facial expression to confirm it.

"I was just down at the Ocean Point Town Hall and I wanted to get your reaction on the protest that is going on." She couldn't help but hope he didn't know. He deserved to have a bomb dropped on him, and she was more than happy to drop it.

"What protest?" His angry tone confirmed her hope. He didn't know.

"You don't know?" Elise asked with as much sweetness as she could muster. It was becoming apparent the phone conversation was going to be even more fun than she had originally thought. Now she was going to be able to get a first reaction quote. And knowing Daniel Johnson it was sure to be a doozy. "There are about thirty residents down there right now carrying picket signs in opposition to your condominium proposal."

"Damn it!"

She looked around the office as she waited for a more printable response. She saw Debbie point her out to someone but she couldn't quite see who it was because of the pole in the center of the newsroom. Elise shifted forward in her desk chair and realized it was Mitch who was asking for her. She held her finger up quickly to let him know she would be with him in a minute.

"I would have thought that this town wouldn't mess with my idea anymore," the developer hissed into her ear. "Especially after everything that's transpired over the past four weeks. How many more people have to be knocked off before they agree to this?"

Was she hearing what she thought she was hearing?

"Meaning?" she asked, curious to see where Daniel Johnson would take his comment.

"Meaning, if this pier gets torn down and we get rid of these damn psychics, maybe the killings will stop."

She strained to hear the quiet, yet angry, words that continued to pour out of the developer's mouth.

"This is your fault, Elise Jenkins. I was told you were asking people a lot of questions after the council meeting last week. You stirred this up, didn't you?"

"I didn't stir anything up. These people have disagreed with your idea from the first time you brought it up last summer. They just want to make sure the council really thinks their decision through before they vote on it at the end of the month," Elise said, defensively.

"They may end up rethinking their *own* decision by the time I'm done," Daniel Johnson said.

The sound of a dial tone filled her ear. She listened to the buzzing for a few seconds before she finally returned the phone to its cradle. Daniel Johnson was on the brink of losing it. And she was afraid he was going to erupt in her direction.

"Elise, you've got a visitor up here!"

*Mitch!*

She jotted down a few remaining notes in her book and then headed up to the reception area.

"Are you okay?" Mitch asked when he saw her.

"I just got off the phone with Daniel Johnson."

"And?"

"Not right now," she said softly.  As much as she loved Debbie, the girl had a big mouth.

"Would you like to grab a bite to eat with me over at the Sidewalk Café?  It's less than six blocks from here."

"Sure.  Just let me get my purse."

She couldn't believe the detective had come to see her, let alone ask her to lunch.  Suddenly, the anxiety she was feeling just moments earlier eased.  Maybe Mitch Burns was semi-interested too.  She walked back to her desk and hit save on her computer.  She didn't want to come back from lunch and find that her picket story had disappeared.

Now she was ready.  She slung her purse over her shoulder and stopped. Karen Smith was talking to Mitch. Elise saw the society reporter hand the detective a folder, say something to him briefly, and then walk away.

"Ready to go," Elise said casually as she joined the detective once again.

When they stepped outside, Elise let out a long, slow sigh.  She hadn't realized just how badly she needed the sunshine and fresh air.

"Tough day?" Mitch asked.

"It wasn't too bad until I spoke to Daniel Johnson.  Excuse me for saying this, but that man gives me the creeps."

"What did he say?"

She related the entire conversation to Mitch as they walked the six blocks to the restaurant.

"He really said all that?"

She nodded, her gaze dropping to her feet.

"He really scares me," she whispered.

"Let me go off the record here for a minute," the detective said, looking into her eyes as they walked.

"The second you asked me to lunch we were off the record, Mitch."

"I gave a lot of thought to what you said about the number one. I varied that angle a little bit and came up with first."

"First?" Her mind began racing in circles as she considered the word. "As in first pier?"

"That certainly went through my mind."

She thought about all the angry things the developer had said to her when she questioned his plan. His whole demeanor suggested the possibility of a horrendous temper. And somehow violent behavior didn't seem like such a big stretch. She shivered.

The feel of Mitch's hand on her arm made her look back up at the detective.

"I'm checking him out, Elise."

"Good."

When they finally reached the restaurant, an attractive waitress led them to a small round table next to a tiny rose bush at the edge of the patio area. She handed them two menus and left. Mitch put his down.

"I'm really sorry that I haven't had much opportunity to talk to you since the other night on the boardwalk," he said. "I really enjoyed the evening with you."

"So did I," she said. Her face grew warm and she looked away briefly. "I can't believe you took the time to walk me home after you got the call about Ben Naismith's murder."

"I wasn't going to leave you there. Besides, I couldn't make you carry that stuffed dog all the way home by yourself, could I?"

She laughed at the thought of the enormous stuffed animal that now graced her tiny bedroom. She had moved the dog out of the entryway after talking to Madame Mariah on the phone the other night in an effort to ward off any troubling dreams. Instead, as she had thought back to her evening with the detective, she had drifted off into the most peaceful night's sleep she'd had in months. But she wasn't ready to share that story with Mitch. Not just yet anyway.

"How are you dealing with all this?" She hadn't meant to ask so quickly, but she couldn't get past the sadness in Mitch's eyes.

"Not very well. I feel like I'm spinning my wheels all the time. I want so desperately to be able to tell the families of the victims that I've caught the man responsible for their deaths. They need that desperately right now."

She looked at him closely and waited. There was an underlying passion in his words that seemed to weigh on him with something even bigger than what was going on in Ocean Point. But she didn't want to pry if he wasn't willing to share.

"When my dad was killed twelve years ago, his death was traumatic for me and my mom. One day he was alive, the next he was dead. But we always knew it was a possibility every time he walked out the door."

"Why was that?" Without thinking, she reached out and covered his hand with hers.

"He was a cop. But what was even harder than his death was the fact that we had no idea who shot him and why. That was what kept my mom awake at night. The gnawing questions and no answers to move on with."

She wanted to move her hand up to his face, stroke away the lines that creased his forehead, but she didn't. Instead, she waited for him to continue.

"One day she simply didn't wake up. She had a massive stroke. But her doctor believed it was brought on by stress. The stress of not knowing. So when the creep who killed my dad fired his gun, he really killed two people with one shot."

"Oh my God, Mitch. You must have been in high school when all that happened." She was horrified at the burden he had been living with for so long.

"I was sixteen when Dad died. Seventeen when Mom died. Aunt Betty took me in, and I managed okay. She was a godsend for me. Her faith got me through most of it. Until just before I moved here." He turned his hand upward and squeezed her hand. "They finally found the bastard who did it. He was a schizophrenic who thought my dad was crossing the street to get him. The cops finally found him because one of his personalities admitted to it at a party one night."

She stared at him, wanting so desperately to comfort him somehow.

"When I came here I almost fell apart myself. I was so angry that it had taken eight years to find the guy. Eight years I lost with my mom. Father Leahy was my saving grace. He and Aunt Betty were rocks that stood by me through some pretty tough times."

It was suddenly so clear to her why Mitch was so protective of her on the boardwalk, why his car was at the station well into the night *every* night. He had given himself a job to do. And it was motivated by an underlying force she was just beginning to understand.

"You're gonna find the person who is doing this, Mitch. You've just got to believe in yourself." She pushed her chair back and walked around the table to him. Leaning down, she wrapped her arms around him and whispered in his ear. "I believe in you."

It was several long moments before he let go. When he did, his face seemed more relaxed, the creases softening on his forehead.

She pointed at the folder he had tucked next to his chair leg. "What did Karen give you?"

"I don't know. She said she had gotten some background information from the chief for a profile article she was doing on him and she asked me to make sure it got back to him."

Mitch opened the folder and looked at the contents inside. Elise noticed the color drain from his face.

"What's wrong, Mitch?"


12:30 p.m.


All the suspicion Mitch had projected onto the chief was for nothing. The boss's file wasn't unusually thin because of some sinister reason. The man had simply given most of the papers to a reporter to help her with a profile.

He shook his head in disgust. He deserved to be strung up by his toenails for believing his boss could be a killer.

"Do you know how long Karen has been working on her profile on Chief Maynard?"

"Probably about a month," Elise answered. She sat back in her chair as the waitress quietly set their water glasses down. "She apparently does an extensive history on everyone she plans to profile so readers can really feel they know the person she is writing about."

"Well, that explains why I didn't see this when I looked at his file."

"What are you talking about?"

"Nothing, now." If it wouldn't make him look like such an idiot, he would consider confessing to his boss. But somehow he knew that the chief wouldn't find Mitch's suspicion to be amusing in the least. And the last thing he wanted was for Elise to think he was a heel, too.

"So what do you think about the possibility that Daniel Johnson may be connected to all of this?" she asked him.

He looked across the table at Elise and smiled. He had never opened up to a woman about his family like he just did. But he wasn't surprised. There was something about her that made him feel alive, yet vulnerable. In a good way.

There were no two ways about it. Elise Jenkins was the kind of girl he had been looking for. Nice, sweet, intelligent, curious. But the timing was bad. He was so wrapped up in work these days he didn't have the time to wine and dine her like he would have liked to. But he had this moment to be with her and he wanted to savor it for as long as possible.

"It sure seems to be growing more likely all the time," he answered quietly.

They ordered their lunch and then sat back to wait. He studied her face as she looked around at their surroundings. She was beautiful. It took everything he had in him not to reach across and move a stray hair away from her blue eyes.

"We got a call today from Ray Carlson," he said, hoping to bring those blue eyes back on him.

"Isn't that the organ player from St. Theresa's?"

"Yeah. And the father of the first murder victim."

"Is he getting angry that the suspect hasn't been caught?"

"He's frustrated, like all of us. But he wanted to inform us that he's posting a $5,000 reward for information that leads to the arrest of the person responsible for these murders."

"Wow," she said. "Thanks for the tip. Maybe a mention of that in Sunday's paper will jog someone's memory."

"That's a good idea. You never know what the promise of cash will do." He leaned back a little so the waitress could set their sandwiches on the table. "Is Scott Levine's funeral tomorrow?"

"Yes it is. Sam is going because he was in a critique group with him."

Mitch nodded his head and smiled at Elise.

"Shall we eat?"

"Definitely."

# 26

## 11:00 a.m.
## Sunday, July 4

It *was a* hard rain.  The kind that made you want to stay indoors with a bowl of soup and a good book.  Certainly not the kind of day the weather forecasters had predicted for the country's birthday.

Elise couldn't help but feel depressed as she sidestepped puddles on the way to St. Theresa's.  All week long she had been looking forward to her first firework display over the beach, and it was obvious the annual event would have to be canceled.

"I wonder how much those television weather people get paid," she mumbled to herself as raindrops pounded her umbrella.  "Whatever it is, it's entirely too much."

As the church's steeple came into view, she could feel her stride getting longer and faster.  It was almost as if her legs understood the mantra running through her head, a constant in her life since childhood.  She could even hear the sound of her mother's voice begging everyone to "eat faster or we'll be late for church".

She had just reached the base of the church steps when she heard someone calling her name.  She turned and saw Mitch walking towards her, his clothes soaked.

"Hi, Mitch."  She knew her smile was huge.  But she didn't care.  She wanted him to know how glad she was to see him.  And not surprisingly, all thoughts of soup and a book magically disappeared from her mind.

"Hi yourself.  Can you spare a few inches under that umbrella until we get inside?" he asked.  "I forgot mine at home."

She moved the umbrella over a few inches and felt him squeeze in next to her.

"Thanks, Elise.  It sure looks as if the Fourth of July fireworks aren't going to happen tonight."  They walked up the concrete steps together. "That means they'll postpone them till Wednesday night."

"Really? I figured they'd just cancel them completely."

"No way. There'd be a mutiny if they did that." He stopped speaking for a moment and cleared his throat. When he continued she could feel his eyes on her. "Want to go watch em' with me?"

She willed herself to remain calm, resist the urge to scream, "Yes!" He was actually asking for a date! When she finally trusted herself enough to speak, her voice was quiet but strong. "I would love to."

Mitch nodded, a self-satisfied grin spread across his face. He winked at her and reached for the church door. But just as she started inside, the sound of running footsteps made her turn.

"Good morning, Mitch. Good morning, Elise." Steve Brown waved his hand in their direction and darted through the set of doors to the right of where they stood.

"That man has the strangest wave I have ever seen," she whispered quietly in Mitch's ear.

"What do you mean?"

"He waves his hand like he's taking some sort of oath. He holds his pinky down with his thumb and then waves." She pushed her thumb down on her bent pinky finger and moved her hand in a direct imitation of the new mayor.

"I've never noticed."

"I noticed it in a picture Dean had of him leaving church a few weeks back," she said. "I'll have to ask him if he knows why the mayor does that."

They each grabbed a bulletin and started down the center aisle that ran between the rows of long wooden pews. She was looking for a place to sit when she felt Mitch's hand on her back.

"Mind if we sit together?" he asked.

"Of course not." She was so totally aware of the feel of his hand on the small of her back that she couldn't think of anything else at the moment. With any luck, no one noticed the huge grin she knew was spreading across her face.

Mitch stopped at a pew and waited for her to sit down first. She set her umbrella on the floor and kneeled for a prayer before the service started. The sudden feel of Mitch's breath next to her ear made her look up.

"Look over there," he whispered, pointing quickly to the right of where they were seated.

"I don't see... Wait a minute. That's Daniel Johnson, isn't it?" she asked softly.

"Yup. I didn't know he was a parishioner here, did you?"

"I didn't either." She could feel her body tense as she looked at the man who had become a source of real fear for her.

"Have you noticed how every single one of the victims was a member of this church?" Mitch asked quietly.

"I didn't really think of it that way, but you're right." She looked slowly around the church. The attendance at St. Theresa's on a regular Sunday resembled that of most churches on a major Christian holiday. "I suppose that could simply be a ratio kind of thing. It seems like an awful lot of people belong to this church."

"I hope you're right."

# 27

## 9:30 a.m.
## Monday, July 5

There was an undeniable feeling of electricity in the conference room that morning as she walked in and sat down. Sunday's paper looked great and Sam beamed like a proud new father.

"Good morning, Elise. Did you have a nice weekend?"

She grinned at her boss as he scooted a small white bag over to her.

"It was fine. But what's this?"

"Breakfast on me," he said. "I know how much you like chocolate, so I got you an east coast favorite."

She reached into the bag and pulled out an oddly decorated cookie. It reminded her of an Asian symbol she had learned about in high school.

"It's called a Black and White. You'll love it."

"Where's mine?" Dean asked as he strode into the room.

"I got one for everybody, don't worry." Sam reached down under his chair and extracted a white bag just like the one in front of Elise.

"To what do we owe this fine honor?" the photographer asked as he pulled out his cookie and broke it in two.

"Sunday's paper was dynamite, so I decided to splurge." Sam reached under his chair once again when Michael and Karen entered the room.

Once everyone was settled and working on a cookie, Sam began the weekly meeting.

"I want to thank you all for a job well done on this weekend's paper. The story on the protest at town hall was exceptional, Elise. The quotes you got were awesome. And those photos you got, Dean—they were the kind of eye-catching shots that make a front page hard to resist."

Elise laughed out loud when she noticed Dean reach over his own shoulder and pat himself on the back. The pretend gun Sam shot in his direction was even funnier.

"The story on Scott Levine's murder was also well done," Sam continued, barely missing a beat after the amusing gesture exchange. "Great job finding out that he, like the others, had consulted Madame Mariah just prior to his death."

"I read that. What's up there?" Dean raised an eyebrow in her direction as his hand dunked a piece of cookie in his coffee mug.

"Madame Mariah called me at home Wednesday night and told me she had seen Scott Levine. She warned him he was in danger, but he thought she was joking." Elise looked around the room at the faces of her coworkers. Everyone looked tired despite Sam's effort to be upbeat. The constant commotion around town was wearing on them all. And the fact that news trucks from across the state were moving into Ocean Point wasn't helping. "She's genuinely concerned for her clients. Think about it...she didn't have to admit to anyone she had seen him. No one would have ever known."

"Do you think she's gotten off the police department's list of suspects?" Dean asked.

"I'm not sure," she answered. "I know she's been cooperative with the police so I imagine she's almost off *their* list, but not necessarily off the list some people have made in their own minds."

"Like Daniel Johnson?" Sam asked pointedly.

"It doesn't help his case if suspicion is turned away from her. He's been using the angle that she is somehow connected with these deaths to move his own agenda through the town council."

She saw Sam nod in agreement then look down at the meeting notes sprawled on the paper in front of him.

"What did the mayor think of the picket the other day?" he asked her.

"He wasn't available for comment. He took the day off to get his parents settled in his home."

"Ever the saint," Dean said sarcastically.

"That reminds me, Dean...I noticed a few weeks ago that you had taken a picture of Mayor Brown as he was leaving church one Sunday." She looked across the table at the photographer who lounged in his seat, one foot on top of the table. "In your picture he was doing a weird wave. Like this."

She held her bent pinky finger down with her thumb and waved her hand with the remaining three fingers extended imitating what she had seen the mayor do the day before. "I saw him do that again yesterday on his way into church. Do you have any idea why he does that?"

"I asked him about that once and he looked at me like I was some sort of pagan." Dean put his foot back down on the ground and crumbled his cookie bag into a ball. "He said that it means to keep holy the Sabbath day."

"What?" She stared at the photographer and waited.

"Evidently that's the third commandment, and like I told you before—he's a religious guru."

"Wow, that *is* odd."

Dean shrugged his shoulders and threw the balled up paper bag in the direction of the wastebasket. It missed.

"Nice to see your aim hasn't improved any," Elise teased, recalling his rotten throw at the dunking booth during the festival.

She saw his tongue shoot out in her direction.

"Okay kids, let's get back to business," Sam said. "I'm sure you've all noticed the white panel trucks with the satellite towers on top. You'd be blind if you didn't notice them on the way in this morning. Our little town has caught the attention of the country it seems, attention that is going to get old very fast." Sam took a quick sip of coffee and paused. "I know my knee-jerk reaction should be to push everyone harder so we don't get shown up by outsiders. But in the same breath, this is our town and this isn't just a *story* for us. I want to keep the momentum we have going."

She was glad to hear him say that. She knew what a circus the press could cause and she didn't want to make her mark in the journalism world that way. She wanted to make it with dignity and compassion. Fortunately, everyone on staff seemed to feel the same way.

"So, what do you have going on this week, Tom?"

The sports reporter snapped to attention and looked down at his notes.

"I've gotten word that a member of the Knicks is going to be on vacation here this week with his family. If my sources pan out and he doesn't cancel with everything going on around here, I should have a pretty good story for next Sunday."

"Do you care to elaborate as to who this player might be?" Dean asked.

"Let me get him first."

"How about you, Karen?" Sam asked, turning his attention to the most difficult staff member.

"I'm wrapping up work on my profile for next Sunday. This one is going to be on a gentleman in town who has some great history to tell about the Ocean Point of yesteryear."

Elise tried to listen politely to Karen, but it was becoming harder and harder to ignore Dean's dramatic yawning from across the table.

"How about you, Dean?" Sam asked, firmly. His disapproving tone was a bad disguise for his obvious amusement over the photographer's antics.

"I'm just gonna do the photojournalism thing this week. Lots of stand alone pictures."

"Elise?"

She sat forward in her chair and looked hopefully at her boss.

"I've been thinking about doing a second part to my fortune teller story. I'm thinking a personal account version with me as the guinea pig could be pretty interesting."

"Great idea. I've always wondered what those psychics really do and interest is certainly at an all time high right now."

Pleased with Sam's reaction to her story suggestion, she looked down at the next idea she wanted to present.

"But, Elise, please be careful."

10:30 a.m.

"Hello, this is Elise Jenkins. May I please speak with Detective Burns?"

She played with the phone chord as she waited, aware of how anxious she was to hear his voice again. The connection she felt to him was so much stronger after their lunch together.

"Detective Burns here."

"Hi, Mitch, this is Elise. I wanted to see if you have any updates for me on the investigations that I can go on the record with."

"Still ongoing, of course. Nothing new at this point but I hope to have something for you very soon."

"I'll check back again with you tomorrow." She was just about to say goodbye when she heard him speak.

"Wait! Are we still on for the fireworks on Wednesday night?" he asked.

The eagerness in his voice was hard to miss.

"Yes, we are. What time do they start?"

"Probably around 9:30, but I thought maybe we could catch a bite to eat beforehand."

The prospect of a date with the handsome detective brought an immediate smile to Elise's lips. She knew that Wednesday couldn't possibly come soon enough.

"Sounds good," she said quietly, hoping that her coworkers weren't eavesdropping. She twirled her pen between her fingers as she tried to think of more things to say to him. "I'm going to be up on the boardwalk tonight."

"Why is that?" he asked quickly.

"I'm going to do a personal account follow-up to my fortune teller story. I'm going to have a reading done and then write about my experience."

"I don't know if that's such a good idea, Elise," the detective said, a note of worry evident in his voice.

She liked the idea that Mitch Burns was worried about her. If he didn't care about her, he wouldn't care what she did. But just the same she was surprised by his obvious concern.

"I don't believe Madame Mariah has anything to do with the murders and I thought you didn't either."

"There must be some sort of connection even if she is innocent," he said.

"If you're worried, why don't you tag along?"

"I would if I could. I'm having dinner with my Aunt Betty tonight. She lives about twenty miles from here and I can't disappoint her."

"She's the woman who took you in after your parents died, isn't she? The one who makes the delicious pies?"

"Yup. That's the one. My mouth is watering already."

"Well, don't worry. I'll be fine," she said. "I better get going now; I've got a lot of work to do. We just got out of our weekly staff meeting and I have a list of stuff I need to get working on for next Sunday's paper."

"Hey, what did your photographer say when you asked him about the mayor's wave?"

"He said that Mayor Brown is reminding people to keep holy the Sabbath day."

"Are you serious?"

"That's what he said," Elise answered. She looked at the clock and reluctantly cut the conversation short. "I'll see you Wednesday night, right?"

"You bet. I'll pick you up at 6:30 if that is okay with you. We can grab a bite, ride a few rides on the pier and then watch the fireworks together on the beach," he said.

"Sounds great. I'll see you then," she said softly. "Goodbye, Mitch."

"Bye, Elise. Please be extra careful tonight."

# 28

The smell of popcorn beckoned as she stepped off the wood plank staircase and onto the boardwalk. It wouldn't be the healthiest dinner she had ever eaten but it certainly wouldn't be the worst.

Elise waited for a break in the throng of people that crossed in front of her, an unwelcome obstacle between her and the old fashioned red popcorn cart a few short yards away. Her stomach gurgled loudly as she looked around at the crowds of people anxious to be out and about after a long, rainy weekend.

It would be fun to meander around the booths and souvenir stands, but she wanted to get to Madame Mariah's as soon as possible. A large crowd surely meant a lengthy wait for the psychic and she was anxious to hear what the woman might say in regards to Elise's romantic possibilities.

The break she was waiting for finally came and she headed straight for the popcorn stand. The smell of the buttery treat was simply more than she could resist.

"I'd like a small buttered popcorn please."

The teenage girl behind the booth stood there and looked at her expectantly.

"You do have popcorn, don't you?" Elise looked at the girl curiously. Why wouldn't she fill the box?

"Yes. But there is no way you're gonna be able to eat this without something to drink. I'd rather get it all at one time."

So much for pleasing the customer. Elise looked at the hand written board next to the cash register and read the limited beverage choices. "How about a bottle of water."

It was all the girl apparently needed. No sooner had Elise finished talking then her box of popcorn and bottle of water appeared on the counter top. The clerk was certainly efficient if not tactful.

"How much do I owe you?"

"Two fifty."

Elise counted out the correct amount of money and handed the cash to the girl. She grabbed the popcorn box and water and turned to go.

"Don't forget some napkins. That butter gets pretty gooey." Elise nodded appreciatively and scooped up a small pile of napkins. Would sticky fingers interfere with a palm reading? She chuckled to herself as she considered the possibility then popped a few fluffy pieces into her mouth. She'd take her chances with sticky fingers.

It was fun to stroll down the pier alone at night. There were so many interesting faces to look at and amusing game vendors to tease back. But she couldn't deny the fact that walking the boardwalk was even more fun with Mitch. And a little scarier without him.

"Want to cook a chicken, miss?"

Not sure if she heard correctly, Elise stopped in her tracks and looked around. A teenage boy motioned her to come over to his booth.

"What's this?" Elise asked. Seven different cooking pots spun around in an overlapping, circular motion.

"Ever played Frog Bog?" the boy asked.

"It's one of my favorites."

"This is just like that, only instead of smacking your frog onto a lily pad, you smack your chicken into the pot."

He held up a brownish colored rubber chicken for Elise to see. Knowing full well that she couldn't resist a challenge, Elise pulled a dollar out of her purse.

"One chicken for a dollar. Three chickens for two bucks."

"This is really a sick game. You *do* realize that don't you?" Elise joked. She reached into her pocket for another dollar bill.

She eyed the rubber chicken the teenager handed her with a mixture of amusement and disgust and plopped it down on the felt-covered ramp in front of her. She positioned the scrawny legs underneath the chicken's body and hit the lever with the mallet. The chicken landed on the floor in front of her.

"The chickens are a little heavier than the frogs," the boy said, an amused grin tugging at his mouth.

"Now you tell me..."

Her second chicken wasn't much better. The third missed a pot by just a few inches.

"Want to try again?"

"Nah, I think I'll stick with the frogs." She took a few steps backward as she spoke, eager to get to the first pier before it got any later.

She felt her back hit something firm behind her. She whirled around and found herself looking into the bewildered face of Mayor Brown.

"I'm so sorry," she said. "I forgot where I was for a second and just backed up while I was talking to the guy behind the counter."

"Not a problem, Elise." Mayor Brown motioned to the young man beside him. "Have you met my son, Jacob?"

She held her hand out to the young man with short brown hair and intense eyes, a younger version of his dad. "Hi, Jacob. I'm Elise Jenkins."

"The reporter?"

The admiration in his eyes surprised her. She knew people read her articles; she just didn't think they would remember her name because of them. "Wow! I didn't think anyone really knew me yet."

"I want to go into journalism too someday, and I read your paper all the time. You're doing a really nice job. I like your style."

"Thanks. That's good to hear once in a while."

"He's right, Elise, you are a very good writer," the mayor interjected.

She could feel her face warming, a sure sign her cheeks were changing color. It was an incredible feeling to realize people not only read what she wrote, but enjoyed it, too.

"It was nice to meet you, Jacob. If you ever want to stop by the paper and look around, give me a call. And I'm so sorry for running into you like that, Mayor."

"No problem. Have a good evening, Elise."

Ten minutes later she finally reached the fortune teller's booth. She tossed a few more pieces of popcorn into her mouth and then threw the rest of the box away. Anticipation over having her fortune told made any lingering hunger disappear.

She walked into the empty waiting room and sat down. The crystals that hung from the ceiling above her head shimmered and sparkled in the muted glow from the moon's light that peeked through the open doorway. She looked around the room for a few more moments, her gaze stopping on the burn marks. The singed wall made her as uneasy now as the first time she saw it. And not surprisingly, she found her thoughts shifting briefly to Daniel Johnson.

"Who's next?" Madame Mariah emerged from behind the red curtain that separated the back room from the waiting area.

"Hi, Madame Mariah." She reached her hand out to the psychic and smiled at her. "I wanted to get a reading from you because I'm curious about what you do. And I think it might make a neat story for the paper."

The woman's gaze traveled the whole length of Elise's body in much the same way it had the first time they met. But this time Elise was comfortable under the apparent scrutiny. She liked Madame Mariah.

When the woman's eyes finally reached Elise's face, she could tell the feeling was mutual.

"Come on back." Madame Mariah held the curtain aside for Elise to walk through.

She stepped into the darkened room and looked around. The dim lighting added to her anticipation.

"Where do I sit?'

"Right there." The woman pointed to a worn red chair beside the tiny round table.

"What do I do?"

"You ask a lot of questions."

"I'm a reporter," Elise answered with a grin.

"Yes, you are. And a very good one I might add," Madame Mariah said. "Would you like a palm reading, Tarot card reading, or shall we take a peek into my crystal ball?"

"How much?"

"For you...nothing. This will be a good opportunity for me to show your readers exactly what I do."

"Could we try all of the different methods if it doesn't get too busy in here?"

"Sure. Let's start with your palm first," the fortune teller said, reaching across the table for Elise's hand.

"What exactly will you be able to see when you look at my palm?"

"I can see things about your career, your goals, your interests. I can see things about your life in general, and I can see into your romantic life as well."

"I was hoping you would say that," Elise said, sheepishly.

"So you want to look at your Heart Line first?"

"I want to, but I'm afraid I won't hear another thing you say after that. So let's look at my career stuff first."

"Head Line it is." Madame Mariah shined the gooseneck lamp onto Elise's palm and bent over it closely.

"You have definitely found your niche in your choice of career. You are being received warmly by the people you deal with in your job. Your writing is going to prove to be a real source of pride for you as you continue to branch out in different directions."

"Directions?"

"I see you writing something in addition to your news articles one day."

"I've always toyed with the idea of trying my hand at a book," Elise said in amazement.

"And you will, but not for a while."

Elise nodded her head in acknowledgement and leaned closer so she could hear the fortune teller's words more clearly.

"Shall we take a look at that Heart Line now?"

"Definitely."

"I see a kind of plateau where nothing has been happening in regards to a romantic relationship," Madame Mariah said. She turned Elise's palm gently and continued speaking.

"But I see that changing. You are getting close to someone you have recently met and you will have a special relationship."

"I was hoping you would say that," Elise said. "I think I know who you might be referring to."

"He will treat you very, very well." She turned Elise's palm once again.

"That's nice to hear..."

"You two will take a trip to a secluded spot and it will prove to be very eventful," the woman said in her trademark cryptic fashion.

"Eventful in a good way or a bad way?"

"Maybe the crystal ball will shed some more light on that for us."

"Is that it for the palm reading?" Elise gently slid her hand out of the fortune teller's loosening grip.

"No." Once again Madame Mariah reached for Elise's hand and gripped it gently. "You have one more main line we must look at and that is the Life Line."

"Okay."

The woman's sudden gasp of fear sent shivers up and down Elise's body.

"What is it?" she asked fearfully. "What do you see?"

# 29

## 8:45 p.m.
## Monday, July 5

"Aunt Betty, that was the best meatloaf I have had in a long, long time." Mitch wiped his mouth with the cloth napkin from his lap and sighed. It felt good to be home. He needed a recharging, desperately.

"I'm glad you enjoyed it, Mitch."

"Let me do the dishes."

"I won't hear of it. I've been looking forward to seeing you for weeks. I'm just going to set them in the sink for now so I can enjoy the rest of your visit."

"I'm sorry again for being so late tonight." He looked at the elderly woman sitting across from him and smiled. Aunt Betty was a grounding force for him. She had stepped into his life without hesitation when Mom died and had been by his side, encouraging him ever since. "Things have been real crazy around the station these past few weeks."

He could see the worried expression in her eyes when she looked at him. She had been so careful to avoid any talk of work throughout dinner and it was just what he needed.

"Would you like some pie? I made your favorite."

"Chocolate cream?"

"That's the one."

"You are so good to me, Aunt Betty." He scooted his chair back a few inches and dropped his hands into his lap. As grateful as he was to her for keeping the dinner conversation light, he needed her advice and encouragement now. But pie could come first.

He waited as she walked briefly into the kitchen and returned just moments later, a large pie plate in her hands.

"I haven't eaten this good since the last time I was here."

"You need to find yourself a good woman," she said, eyeing him curiously.

"I know, I know."

His thoughts went to Elise...their time together on the boardwalk, their lunch together the other day, their upcoming date on Wednesday...

"You've met someone, haven't you?"

"This is *so* good," Mitch said, pointing to the pie. He liked Elise Jenkins a lot, but he wasn't ready to share too much information about her just yet. Especially not with Aunt Betty, of all people. She could be such a pitbull on the subject.

"Don't you change the subject on me, Mitchell. Who is she?"

He hadn't heard her call him Mitchell in years. And just as it had worked when he was a young boy, he found himself answering her question.

"Her name is Elise Jenkins. She's the new reporter over at the Ocean Point Weekly."

"I want to meet her."

"Aunt Betty, I've only talked to her a few times myself. I've been really busy at work lately," he said helplessly. He knew his aunt well enough to know she wasn't going to let the possibility of a girlfriend go. She had never liked being left out of anything.

"What's she like?"

"She's very, very sweet. And very, very pretty." His thoughts trailed off again.

"You're smitten with her, aren't you?"

"I don't really know. We went on the boardwalk together one evening and then to lunch one day last week. Oh, and we sat together at church on Sunday."

"Good. She's a churchgoer."

He looked fondly at the woman sitting across the table from him. Aunt Betty had a one track mind when it came to church and her nephew finding a good woman.

"She seems to be a really nice person. We're going to the fireworks together on Wednesday night."

"Good...good."

He smiled to himself as he watched Betty's eyes sparkle from behind her thick glasses. She was plotting and he knew it.

"When do I get to meet her?"

"Aunt Betty, I really haven't spent much time alone with her myself. Things have been crazy for both of us at work...I'm just glad that she was able to overlook my rudeness in the beginning."

"Mitchell! Why were you rude to her?"

"I didn't mean to be. These murders are really frustrating. I've got a lot of people relying on me to solve these cases and bring this lunatic to justice."

"I read that each of the victims had consulted a fortune teller prior to their death," she said.

"That's right."

"You wouldn't catch me anywhere near a fortune teller."

Mitch looked at his aunt closely, surprised by her comment.

"Why not?"

"Because it's a sin."

"What are you talking about?" His mouth went dry, his heart rate quickened as he waited for her to explain.

"It's breaking a Commandment. When you consult a psychic, you are saying that you believe they can see the future. But as Christians we are taught that God alone knows the future, no one else." He felt his mouth drop open as the meaning of her words hit him right between the eyes.

"The *First* Commandment..."

"That's right."

"Oh my God," Mitch said in horror as he stood up and ran for the telephone in his aunt's kitchen.

# 30

9:15 p.m.
Monday, July 5

"Elise, I see near tragedy for you. You must be very, very careful when you leave here tonight."

She stared at the fortune teller, too shocked to speak. It had to be a joke, didn't it? But she knew it wasn't. The fear in Madame Mariah's eyes told her it wasn't.

"Is it...is it like you saw for the victims?"

"Yes. Just like that."

"Why is this happening?" Her voice cracked and grew hoarse.

"All I can say is that you are breaking the law and you will face punishment," Madame Mariah said gravely.

"What law am I breaking?"

"A law composed by a higher power."

"I'm scared, Madame Mariah."

"So am I, Elise. You must go home now, and lock your door. Be very careful."

She nodded slowly, unsure of where to go and what to do. She couldn't call Mitch. He was at his aunt's house. Dean was at a party and Sam had a writer's meeting. There was no one.

Elise breathed in slowly, willed herself to remain calm. It was the only way to think clearly. She squeezed the fortune teller's hand and walked out onto the boardwalk.

The crowds that had milled around earlier were all but gone. Now, when she looked down the boardwalk, all she could see were empty booths that provided a great place for someone to hide behind. She turned and looked at the beach. The foamy waves glowed in the moonlight. It was wide open.

Elise crossed the boardwalk and walked down the short flight of stairs onto the beach.  She hoped that the fresh ocean air would help clear her mind.

"Breaking the law...breaking the law...breaking the law..."

Maybe by repeating the fortune teller's words over and over she might be able to make some sense of them.

"...a law composed by a higher power..."

*God?*

"Could she mean God?" Elise said aloud, listening to the way the word sounded as it escaped her mouth and disappeared in the sound of the crashing waves.

*Laws composed by a higher power...*

"Laws composed by God..."

She slapped her hand over her mouth as the pieces began to fit for the first time.  The Commandments are God's law.

"How am I breaking the Commandments by going to see Madame Mariah?" she shouted into the darkness.  But no one answered.

She reached for her cellular phone and dialed information.

"What town, please?"

"Ocean Point."

"What listing?"

"St. Theresa's rectory."

"Would you like me to connect you straight through?"

"Please!"

The phone rang once and was answered.

"Good evening, St. Theresa's."

"Father Leahy.  This is Elise Jenkins."

"Hello, Elise.  You sound troubled."

"Is it breaking a Commandment to see a fortune teller?"

"That's strange. I just got off the phone with someone who asked me that very same question."

"Is it?"

"Yes it is, Elise. The First Commandment says we shall not have strange Gods before Him. God alone knows the future. By believing in a psychic's ability to see the future, we are giving him or her a perfection which belongs only to God."

"Thank you, Father." She blinked hard against the stinging tears in her eyes.

"Are you okay, Elise?"

"I've got to go, Father.  Good night."

She shut the cellular phone and slipped it back into her pocket, her mind reeling in a million directions. Each one of the victims had been a member of St. Theresa's. They had broken the First Commandment. *She* had broken the First Commandment.

"Oh my God, the *First* Commandment," she shouted. "All of the victims had their index finger extended as if saying the number one...the First Commandment..."

Horrified by the thoughts in her head, Elise stopped in her tracks. Snatches of conversation ran through her mind, rewinding and playing at will.

> ..."A prayer for the poor parents." Not the victims themselves.
> ... "Fortune tellers are imposters."
> ... "Honor Thy Father and Mother"...
> ..."Keep Holy the Sabbath Day"

Over and over she heard his words, his voice. He had seemed so sincere, so genuine in his faith and concern. Why hadn't she been able to see him the way Dean had? She looked down at her hand as she mimicked the wave she had seen less than 36 hours ago.

> ...Keep Holy the Sabbath Day is the Third commandment...that's why he waves with three fingers up!

Elise stumbled across the sand as she realized the enormity of what was happening. She wiped futilely at the torrent of tears that streamed down her face.

The sound of muted footsteps behind her brought her sobs to a dead stop. She knew without a shadow of a doubt that he was behind her, ready to punish her for her sin. Just as he had punished all the rest. She turned slowly, her feet dragging in the sand, until she could see into his angry face.

"You sinner! You must be punished!"

"Please, don't," she screamed. She saw the wooden object in his hands as he raised his arms into the air. She recognized the stained and battered wood. It had been hanging in his office all along.

"You are just like all of them..."

"Who?" she asked, taking several steps backward, hoping to gain some distance between them.

"Susie, Cindy, Ben and Steve. You all go to church on Sunday morning and act like you are such good followers..."

"I am. They were..."

"Liar!" he screamed. "Thirty-six hours after you worshipped in His house, you were all asking that imposter to tell you things that only God can know!"

"I didn't know it was a sin," she pleaded.

"You should have known! And now you must pay, just as they did!" He pulled his arms back, stared at her with open hatred.

"No!" She turned and ran toward the boardwalk lights that seemed so far away.

She tripped on the soft, dry sand and fell to her knees. There was no use. He had her right where he wanted her.

"Please don't kill me..."

"I liked you, Elise." Steve Brown relaxed his grip on the cross and looked at her with pity. "You seemed to have such high morals and convictions, but I was wrong..."

"I *do* have high morals. I honestly didn't know that going to a fortune teller was a violation of the Commandments, you have to believe me," she pleaded, her words ending in gut wrenching sobs.

"You should have known," he said angrily as his grip tightened once more on the piece of wood in his hands.

She saw his arms raise in the air, saw them come back towards her head. Elise closed her eyes and said a quick prayer.

The sound of a gunshot ripped through the quiet night like a clap of thunder. Elise heard a low, guttural moan that wasn't from her own mouth. She opened her eyes and saw Mayor Brown falling face down in her direction, the weapon he was holding still grasped tightly in his hands.

With a sudden burst of energy, Elise rolled to the side just as the man's body hit the sand where she had been.

Bewildered, she looked in the direction the gunshot had come from. The light from the moon shone down like a spotlight on Mitch Burns.

She sank down into the sand and began crying uncontrollably. In an instant the detective was at her side, cradling her in his arms.

"It's okay, Elise. Everything is okay, now," he whispered soothingly into her ear. She could hear the worry in his voice and feel the relief in his arms.

"How did you know?" she asked him when she was finally able to speak.

"My aunt told me about the First Commandment. I called Father Leahy for confirmation." His lips brushed briefly across her forehead, lingered on her temple. "I'm just glad I got here in time."

"So am I."

# 31

## 10:30 a.m.
## Wednesday, July 7

*She was tired* but ready.  She wanted to reclaim her life and move on. And returning to work was the first step.

She inhaled deeply, savoring the salty sea air and the bright July sun that left little room for clouds of doubt.  She pushed open the door and stepped inside.

"Oh my God, Elise...it is sooo good to see you," Debbie said as she came from behind her desk to give Elise a quick hug.  "Are you okay?"

"Yeah, I really am."  The receptionist's warm embrace was just the added reassurance she needed at that moment.  It really was going to be okay.

"Hey, everybody...Elise is back," Debbie yelled.

"Deb, you don't have to..."

Before she could finish her sentence, Elise saw Sam jogging toward her.

"Are you okay?"  The worry in his face was touching.  She reached out and squeezed her boss's hand.

"I'm okay, Sam."

"Detective Burns stopped by first thing yesterday morning and told us what happened."  She could feel him looking her over from head to toe, could sense the questions he wanted to ask but didn't.  "He said you needed to take the day off and relax. Doctor's orders."

"Mitch insisted I go to the hospital after everything happened, even though I was perfectly fine, physically.  The doctors said I had been through quite an emotional ordeal and they felt I should stay home and get some rest."

"Absolutely," Sam said.  He put an arm around her shoulder and guided her towards his office.

"They were right, because I spent almost all of yesterday sleeping." She sat down in the chair across from her boss's desk. "I've never been so tired in my life."

"I just can't believe that Mayor Brown could be so off keel." It was funny but even after everything she knew, she still felt some of the disbelief she saw in Sam's eyes.

"I told you he was nuts."

Elise looked up and saw Dean standing in the doorway of Sam's office. Nodding in grudging acknowledgement, she took a second to compose her words.

"That you did. But as any good journalist knows, the photo only tells half the story. You need the written part to really get the truth." She wanted desperately to get back to some semblance of normalcy and trading barbs with Dean was a good place to start.

"That 'written part' as you call it, could have gotten you killed," Dean said, an uncharacteristic softness evident in his voice.

"You sound as if you care, Dean."

"I do. But if you tell anyone around here that I said that, I will deny it like there's no tomorrow."

"Deal."

"I guess I'm in on the secret, too," Sam said.

"What secret?" Dean asked.

"Hey, Elise, you got a delivery up here," Debbie shouted from the front of the building.

"Somebody's got to get that girl an intercom so we can keep our hearing a little bit longer." Dean smacked the side of his head playfully and stuck a finger in his ear.

Pushing Dean to the side of the doorway so she could get by, Debbie strode into Sam's office with a small but tasteful flower arrangement. The bright, cheerful flowers brought an instant smile to Elise's lips.

"Those are for me?" she asked, as Debbie placed the flowers carefully in her lap.

"Yup."

She didn't need the envelope to tell her who they were from.

"Don't keep us in suspense here," Dean said, covering his mouth over a dramatic yawn.

"Let's give her some privacy guys." Sam scooted Dean and Debbie out of the office and then looked back over his shoulder at her. "I'm glad you're okay."

"Thanks, Sam," she said softly. Once she was finally alone, she pulled the envelope off the flower arrangement and opened the seal.

*I wanted you to know that I was thinking about you today and hoping that you are okay. See you tonight at 6:30.*

The card was signed, *Mitch.*

It looked as if Madame Mariah was right about the budding relationship with a man she had recently met. She reached across Sam's desk for the telephone and dialed the now-familiar number.

"Ocean Point Police Department."

"May I speak with Detective Burns please?"

"Who's calling?"

"Elise Jenkins."

Less than two seconds later she heard the sound of his voice. A voice she would remember for the rest of her life.

"You got them?"

"I got them. And they're beautiful."

"I was hoping that they would help brighten your day."

"They did. And so did you."

"Good, I'm glad. How are you feeling this morning? Did you get some good rest?"

She twirled the phone cord around her index finger and closed her eyes. The concern in the detective's voice was unmistakable, touching.

"I feel better, thanks. I did wake up once during the night, feeling rather ashamed of myself."

"Ashamed? Why?"

"Ashamed of passing judgment on Daniel Johnson and thinking he was a murderer."

"Elise, we didn't know *who* was doing this. Johnson's aggressive attitude and threats certainly didn't help his case any."

"I guess you're right."

"I am. So stop worrying, okay?"

"Okay." Elise sat back and looked around Sam's office, her gaze coming to rest on a framed picture of Ocean Point's amusement piers and boardwalk. "Do you think he'll finally get his luxury condos?"

"I don't know. But I think the whole topic will be put on the back burner for awhile. People need to heal first. It's been a tough month in Ocean Point and I think everyone needs to return to a little bit of normalcy if that's possible."

"I agree."

She looked at the card in her hand and at Mitch's name scrawled across the bottom and smiled. She'd finally found a true gentleman.

"Elise? Are you still there?"

"Yeah, I'm here."

"Are we still on for tonight?"

"There's no place I would rather be," she said honestly.

"Me neither. I'll pick you up at 6:30."

"Sounds perfect."

"Want to eat at Mia's?" he asked.

"I would love to."

It was obvious that the detective was glad she had called. In fact, it seemed as if he was reluctant to let her go.

"So, what's on tap for you at work today?"

"I'm going to work on my story about the other night..."

"Are you ready for that, Elise?"

"As ready as I'll ever be."

"I know something that might make you feel a little better."

"What's that?" she asked.

"Remember how I told you that Ray Carlson had posted a $5,000 reward for information leading to the arrest of his daughter's murderer?"

"Yes."

"He wants you to have it."

"Mitch, I can't take that from him," she said emphatically.

"He wants you to have it...and you deserve it. Use it for a vacation, you've certainly earned one."

"You deserve that money every bit as much as I do," she argued gently.

"If you use the money to go on a trip, you can take me with you."

She thought of Madame Mariah's prediction about an eventful trip to a secluded spot. She just hoped it wasn't too eventful.

"You're on."

"I'll hold you to that," the detective said. "I'll let you go now so you can write your story. If you need anything before tonight, give me a call. Otherwise I'll see you at 6:30."

"Thanks, Mitch."

She set the phone down and walked out into the newsroom. Her computer was waiting for her. She pushed the small power button on the base of the machine and watched as the screen came to life. It was time to relive Monday night all over again. And then she could finally put it behind her...for good.

She positioned her fingers on the keyboard and began typing, her hands taking over as the words seemed to pour out of them and onto the screen in front of her.

*Deeming himself judge and jury, Ocean Point Mayor Steve Brown set about the task of handing down verdicts on people he saw as criminals. It was in his pursuit of justice that he himself stumbled on the law. By punishing his victims for breaking the First Commandment, he was guilty of breaking one himself.*

*The Fifth commandment says, "Thou Shalt not Kill."*

While drawing scenes at a friend's house in the fifth grade, Laura Bradford fell in love with the idea of writing picture books for children. The fun of creating characters and plots—coupled with artwork—was the "it" she'd been searching for.

From that moment on, Laura set her sights on being a writer and never looked back. Every opportunity to write was snatched up—from a Girl Scout troop newsletter in sixth grade, to a creative writing class in eighth grade, to movie reviews for her college newspaper—with each experience reinforcing her desire to become a writer.

The summer after her freshman year of college, Laura took an internship at a weekly newspaper in New Milford, Connecticut. Her boss took her under his wing and taught her everything about leads, interviews, and an ending that resonated long after the story was gone.

Graduation from college brought reporting jobs as she moved around with her husband, a helicopter pilot in the U.S. Army. After he left the military, they settled in the St. Louis area where Laura worked as a news reporter for the O'Fallon Journal.

When her first daughter was born, Laura hung up her news reporter hat and focused on motherhood...dabbling in occasional freelance work for the newspaper and area businesses.

After her second daughter was born, a good friend helped re-ignite her childhood passion for writing fiction. But this time it was in the area she enjoyed reading most...mysteries.

And that's when *Jury of One*, and the characters of Elise Jenkins and Mitch Burns, were born.

Now, Laura's news reporter hat belongs to Elise. And Mitch, well, he's a little bit of the many great police officers and emergency workers Laura worked with over the years. The characters' town—a small beachside community in Laura's own native New Jersey—allows her to write about another passion...the beach!

To learn more, visit Laura at her website: www.laurabradford.com

Printed in the United States
55924LVS00003B/64

9 781591 330943